Perfect Union

Chapter One

"You can only soldier on when you have purpose and fortitude to do so. Without united purpose, without united hope, and without united values our mission for sustainability will fail and we will become weak and

divided." General Sean Bishop

<u>U.S. Presidential Address- London Peace Summit</u>

The mumbling sound of a large crowd filled the arena. Large indirect fluorescent lights provided an ambient glow through the large room. The tapping on the microphone brought a hush to the crowd. Secretary of State, Alvin Tyler, smiled as President Stanley Brimley walked up to him and stood by his side as they waited to be announced from the wing of the stage. The President extended his hand to Mr. Tyler and gave a firm handshake.

"Good to see you Mr. Tyler." The President pleasantly said.

"Good to see you Mr. President. I'm proud to be here."

Prime Minister Sheffield turned towards the President from the podium to introduce him.

"Ladies and Gentlemen, the President of the United States of America!"

President Brimley glanced back at his Secretary of State.

"That's us, let's go." The President acknowledged taking a two-step lead in front of Secretary of State Tyler. The President's smile beamed widely as he walked toward the podium among a scattering of cheers.

The nervous Secretary of State following the President wiped a bead of sweat from his brow. He then discreetly withdrew a Beretta M9 Army service pistol from his coat pocket as they approached the podium. The Secretary of State hid the gun from view as he accompanied the President of the United States. His step was quick, and he was focused. Without hesitation, Alvin Tyler lined the gun to the Presidents head and fired off 3 quick rounds. The President collapsed to the stage. His body lies in a pool of blood, lifeless before a screaming crowd of horrified onlookers.

My parents thought of me as a dreamer. Well, I should say my mother did as she seemed to catch me daydreaming and would have to remind me to study and do my homework as a youth. Dad enjoyed the fact that he had a boy to play catch with and hoped I would take over the family farm one day. Dad just wasn't sure about me. I think that comes from the fact that I just didn't want to go into the family dairy farming business. I kind of always thought of myself as a late bloomer.

Anyway, my name is Beauregard Brown. Beauregard is of French origin meaning "beautiful gaze". I never really liked the name. My friends call me Bo. I am a thirty-two-year-old former financial analyst from New York City. I grew up in the majestic hills of West Virginia. In the last five years the experiment in power and democracy formally known as the United States has failed. It has been ravaged by a civil war that could not be reconciled. History has failed this once great nation where leaders once stood tall and delivered fabled speeches like the Gettysburg Address. Those leaders have now eluded us and all but disappeared into an abyss of corporate greed, elitism, nationalism, and war brought about by selfish tyranny and government disfunction. A tyrannical fascist by the name of Gerald Hughes claimed the Presidency by force and caused such government dysfunction that the government infrastructure we once took for granted has fallen. Our great institutions that are the pillars of justice, economy, health, defense, and welfare have degraded to bully pulpits and failure. There were pockets of democracy in the west and the far south. Many people perished, fled, or became indifferent to the fact that life failed them. I have been fighting along with others for survival and hope. This is my story.

My family's farm was once a placid scene with nothing but acres of rolling hills of green grass with a stand of large peach trees and the scent of fresh pine and peach blossoms from the nearby hills. The mornings were my favorite as the dew on the grass and honey suckle brought back feelings of youth and innocence. My dad would sip a glass of iced tea in the afternoon on the large front porch of the main house, now abandoned. It was a great place to grow up. The farm was a complex of old buildings along with new. As a child I enjoyed playing in the small old barn and amongst the peach trees in the small orchard adjacent to the main house. There was also a milking facility built on the property about a hundred yards from the old barn. I loved West Virginia but I grew intolerant of some of the folks I grew up with that seemed to surround me. I suppose maybe Mom was right, I was a dreamer. A dreamer that hated the ignorance of a nation that I thought should know better.

The artificial boundary lines of the states are still represented if nothing else by the hope and loyalty of those that once called these places home. As I walk along an abandoned roadway with scores of others, I find a strange comfort amongst the pain and anguish of other refugees. I was not the only one longing for peace, for a sense of normalcy, for a sense of calm, and for a sense of a time that may never be again. I often think and ask myself, can the values of freedom, peace, family, and the search for happiness ever have the capability to reform a new Union.

No one knew what the truth of a Union was anymore. No one knew what contentment, national pride, or leadership was anymore. It was a lost and fleeting feeling.

I often smell the stench of chemicals, mixed with smoke and embers among the war ruined wasteland. Anguish seems to consume all.

I stopped my long walk briefly to turn and check on the old man that was walking behind me. He stood looking to the ground and clinging onto his long walking stick. He gasped quickly to catch his breath.

"Are you ok my friend?" He was nothing but a stranger to me.

He slowly raised his head. He was dirty and disheveled from the long journey. His eyes were crystal blue but set deep against his dirty face. His greying thin hair blowing in the soft smoky breeze.

"I'm as well as I can be, I suppose." He responded by shaking his head.

I walked back to him to see if there was anything I could do to ease his suffering.

"How old are you, my friend?"

The man raised his head and looked at me with a slim smile.

"Seventy-one."

"You've done well for yourself old man." I responded with a wink and a smile. A small conciliation on a miserable day.

We paused as we looked around us. There were people migrating in long lines, side by side, all slowly making their way to their unknown destinies.

"Do you see that old tree line over there my friend?" I asked the old man as I pointed beyond a small hill.

He gazed and shook his head in the affirmative fashion.

"That is the edge of my family's property. I am the only one of my family that remains. I feel it is my responsibility to see what's left. I'm not sure what brings me back here."

"A sense of home, perhaps?" He asked.

We started walking again slowly side by side. Like many others, on a path to a lost place in our hearts, most of us head south for the winter and to escape gang warfare. I turned and looked at the man.

"My name is Bo."

The man looked up at me, "My name is Thomas", he replied as he shook my hand.

"Nice to meet you, Thomas. Do you mind if I walk with you a bit?" I asked, attempting to ease the old man's obvious loneliness and discomfort.

"Not at all young man."

"I'm going to make my way over to that nearby tree line. From there is an old dirt road that leads to the main house. Please walk with me Thomas."

The man walked along with me at a slow pace. I enjoyed his quiet company. It was as if I'd known this old man for a long time when it's only been minutes. That's how it is now. Time doesn't seem to have relevance. The days are painful and the nights endless. The people you meet are fleeting and typically hopeless and adrift seeking something elusive.

The quiet didn't last long. A shout and squabble could be heard coming from down the hill. We could see a gang of young men dragging a young girl into some nearby brush. She struggled frantically. Suddenly, gun fire rang out from some nearby rescuers and the men fled.

Thomas looked at the scene intently.

"Animals!" He said in disgust.

"The world has collapsed to nothing but animals!" he repeated.

I watched the scene as the mother grabbed her young daughter and began running to get her away from the scene. Some others came to their aid and swept them into a small group to protect and cuddle the girl. Rape had become common in this lawless land.

I have become almost immune to chaos, crime, and insanity. To think that it has come to this is very disheartening.

Thomas and I made it to a familiar place in my past. The large tree still stood. A boulder that I had played on as a child stood sentinel over the grand slopping hill that overlooked this West Virginian farm. I stopped and gazed at the scenery.

"Thomas, let us sit here upon this rock for a moment and rest."

Thomas gently put his long walking stick upon the rock and found himself a comfortable seating place. I sat beside him.

"I won't ask what side you were on." Thomas said as he gazed straight ahead.

I looked at the older man and started to smile at him.

"I stopped taking sides a long time ago my friend." I said.

"I am now on the side of survival. I just want peace and to survive."

"Isn't that what everyone wants son?" He replied.

"No Thomas, it's not." I replied. "There were those that wanted power. Hell, there are those that still seek control and power. I will never understand most of it."

"There is little to no control left to have." The man said as he looked at me.

"When the Freedom Party took power, I knew the end was near. In any event it doesn't matter now. I hope they are all in hell." He said with no remorse.

I reminded Thomas, "The Freedom Party started as a political action group that used the religion, beliefs, and idealism of others to cater to their own needs. Tell the masses what they want to hear, get their full backing, reward, reinforce, and conquer."

Thomas just looked at me and shook his head. "No one understood." Thomas said.

I looked at the main house down the hill and tried to catch a scent of the late summer honey suckle. It was not the same.

"I take it you were not in the Freedom Party or with their regime?" I asked Thomas.

Thomas laughed. "Actually, I was!" He said with a chuckle.

"There is nothing better than to know that you have been forgiven and believing in a higher power that can get you through any situation. And it's not just that. I sought what I thought was a way of life that I missed, that I thought was being taken from me. I take it you are not?" He asked me.

"Thomas, look around you. What do see? Nothing but lonesome beat-up souls searching for what? They have no idea. Does this look like freedom? I never understood the Freedom Party. I take that back. I do understand the party now, power and tyranny. The strife has taken its toll, hell no I'm not with the insurgency, I'm with the Union. It is time to move past all the crazy ideologies and become one people again. A people that can believe in one free land where you can strive for happiness, love, and hold on to sanity. I think we all want the same thing. Somehow our country became divided and lost. What happened to those credence's Thomas?" I asked.

"I don't know my friend." Thomas said with a smile.

I thought about what he said for a minute and looked at him. He just smiled at me and stood up to continue the journey.

"War; my friend, is started by a few, but fought by many." I said as I began my walk toward my old home.

"It is troubling to me how I see many following the few." Thomas said.

"That is very true Thomas and something we can both agree on! Remember, it was never about freedom. It was never about faith. It was never about morality. It was never about making a great God-fearing country or a great economy. It was about power. Always was and always will be." I said.

At this point I became complacent about my past and beliefs. The argument is over. It was over a long time ago, at least for me. But I still dream, and I will still fight.

The rest of the walk down the hill was quiet except for the occasional scream from a nearby hillside of someone being robbed, beaten, or raped. A common consequence of the war, and roving gangs. An occasional gun shot rang out.

I approached my old home cautiously with Thomas. Not a pane of glass was left in the windows. The rain gutters hung down broken and battered by the elements. The front door was half open, apparently only hanging by a few loose screws. The large front porch where my father sat once, happily sipping iced tea was now a heap of battered wood decking. My mind raced against the memories lost to time. I had to come back to the here and now. We needed fresh water.

"Hello?" I yelled out not to startle any wrong doers.

Not a sound came from the house. I still approached cautiously.

"Stay back Thomas." I said, waving my hand.

I carefully watched my footing so not to fall through the broken decking. I slowly pushed the door open for a better look inside.

"Hello?" I yelled out again but sensed no one.

As I walked inside, I could see the familiarity of the rooms. Ragged drapery hung blowing in the gentle breeze through the open house. No pictures were on the walls, no furniture was immediately seen.

"Come on in Thomas!" I cautiously said.

I gently took off my backpack that contained all my worldly possessions and put it on the floor. I peeked into the kitchen expecting to see my mother cooking soup on the stove. I saw no stove, just a bare wall where once the stove sat.

I turned to look for Thomas and made my way to assist him.

"Hey Thomas!" I yelled to him eager to show off my old haunt. I again, turned to look for him.

Within a quick breath I stood at the threshold of my home and found the old man with a crossbow and cocked arrow pointed at his temple. Three young dirty men stood around him. Their demeanor was of desperation. The man holding the cross bow begin to quiver as sweat fell from his dirty face.

"Please!" I yelled at the men.

"We are not a threat and we have just journeyed a long way. Put the bow down and we will leave peacefully." I pleaded.

With no thought to his actions the young man suddenly launched the arrow clean into Thomas's temple. The bow's impact made a thud sound as it hit his head with tremendous force as the point protruded through to the opposite side of his head. Blood spattered on one of the men standing nearby. I watched Thomas drop to the ground. The man had no life left in him at the gentle age of seventy-one. His piercing blue eyes gave one last look of desperation before his head hit the floor.

Without thought, I quickly took cover behind the door. I reached for my backpack lying close by. My hand found my .357 magnum. I pointed and fired off several rounds into the door not even knowing what was on the other side. There was no movement. I heard no sound. Only the smoke from my gunfire and scent of gunpowder filled the air. I swung the door back exposing myself, quickly got to my feet and peered out the open window. The men were gone. I glanced at Thomas as he lay motionless on the ground with an arrow through his head. Blood pooled around his thin gray hair. I went to his side. There was nothing I could do. I realized I knew nothing about this dead man other than the fact his name was Thomas; he was seventy-one and he had once been in the Freedom Party. Something I sensed he had long regretted; not his faith, but his affiliation with and the following of those that got us to this point. I just shook my head and felt weary. Another senseless act. I can't keep count anymore the senseless actions of mankind and how many times I've asked myself why.

The war came at great cost as all wars do I suppose. The idealistic reasoning behind the slaughter of millions was animalistic and evil. I sat down in my former place of peace and happiness next to the dead old man with my back against the wall. I began to cry in my exhaustion.

<u>Looking back</u>

"Bo, I need your opinion! Wait! Quit walking so fast! Where are you off to?" Austin asked as he tried to keep my pace.

"Austin, I'm trying to finish up a project. My Dad wants me to come home this weekend to help around the farm." I spoke.

Austin stopped me and gave me a stupid look.

"Right! You like going back to that farm about as much as I like visiting my alcoholic mother in Queens!"

Austin Finch thought he knew me. Of course, he really didn't. He was a young up and coming conservative idealist that escaped his mother's alcoholic wrath when he turned 18. He was bright enough to find a scholarship to put himself through the University of New York School of Business and Finance and end up here at Harcroft & Harrison Consulting working with me developing portfolios for other, wealthier up and coming spoiled idealists. Despite his shortcomings, he still became a good and loyal friend. He just likes to paint me as someone I'm not.

My idea of success came rather early. My father established and worked a large dairy farm and my mother worked as a microbiologist in the neighboring town attempting to find ways to improve milk production among cows. It was a struggling cause and a slow business since the increased use of plant based and other artificial milk products pushed them out of the cow milk industry. Dad saw an opportunity to use the farm space as a production plant for the plant-based milk and

Mom became very successful in the development of a high nutrition milk product based on bee honey and soy. Don't ask me how but the combination of the two of them made for a very successful team.

I loved my home, I loved my folks farm, and of course I loved my folks, but as any young man with fire in his eyes and hope in his heart I ventured away from our West Virginia farm to New York to attend college. Despite my father wanting me to take over the farm and artificial milk business someday I just didn't have the passion to follow that path. Besides, I knew nothing nor cared anything about the artificial milk business. Plant based or not; there were just too many other supplements and fads to take its place. My degree in business and finance took me in another direction.

My relationship with Austin Finch is a friendship that started instantaneously through a passion for sarcasm and college beer drinking. We both sustained a love of family. Despite the raging turmoil an alcoholic parent can bring, Austin seemed to survive it well and if not for his own independent and strong-willed nature he may not have survived it at all. His father was a strong conservative that only saw God as the salvation for his family and for Austin's life. Fortunately, Austin had other plans.

We both ended up applying and working for the same company in upstate New York at a rather large business and tech firm called Harcroft & Harrison Consultants. A liberal company run by mostly women with a theme of caring and love to customers as well as employees. We felt lucky to work there.

I like to work in the multimedia and marketing aspect of the company attempting to grow and develop businesses. I thought I had found a niche.

"Austin, let me compile and enter this last page of data and I will be right with you." I told Austin as he eagerly awaited over my shoulder.

I could feel Austin's presence hovering over me relentlessly.

"Seriously Austin, I need about an hour! What is your problem?"

"I think I'm in love man." Austin mumbled.

"What?" I asked, making sure I heard him correctly.

"I'm in love with Francesca." he said, sheepishly.

I paused, turned, and gave my friend a big smile. "Wow! That's awesome man! She's a great lady." I said to give my approval.

I barely knew Francesca, having only met her twice.

"It's about time you have somebody to settle your ass down." I said.

I gave Austin a pat on the shoulder and smiled.

"So, what do you need my opinion on?" I asked.

"I just want to make sure I'm doing the right thing man." He said.

"The right thing? Of course, you're doing the right thing!"

I felt my advice to Austin was nothing more than a mere vote of confidence.

"Austin, you're doing the right thing! You have my full support and I look forward to being at the wedding but right now I'm very sorry I must run."

With that said I finished up my report to management, sent it off in an email and headed out the door to sneak in a quick happy hour meeting with Quintero Rodriquez.

Quintero was a former coworker of mine who had called me several times to set up this meeting. I finally owed it to him. Quintero was also a radical. Some would call him a very left-wing socialist nut, but I tended to like him and thought he had a big heart. He also had just recently become divorced, so I thought maybe he needed someone to talk to.

I sat patiently waiting at a high-top table overlooking 54th Avenue. It was the month of May, so the weather was perfect, and a cool pleasant breeze blew the sounds of the city streets up to the open lounge terrace.

"Nothing like New York City." I said to myself as I sipped a cold beer.

I liked New York. It was a far cry from the farmland of West Virginia as it was a pleasant change and brought about a quick pace of life that I enjoyed.

I wasn't halfway through my beer when in walked Quintero.

"Hello, my friend!" he said as he reached around and gave me a hug.

He appeared to be happy and had a smile on his face. I thought this could be a cover, but I'll hear him out.

"Quin it's very good to see you! So, what's going on?" I asked, getting right to the point even though he had yet to order a drink.

"A lot is going on my friend! Let me grab a bourbon and we'll talk! We have some catching up to do!" He said as he flagged down a waitress.

"Bo, have you ever heard of the Freedom Manifesto?"

"No Quintero, what conspiracy theory are you researching now?" I asked suspiciously.

"I don't believe this to be a conspiracy my friend. I believe the war between the left and the right is coming to a head. The Freedom Manifesto is an Ultra-Right-Wing Manifesto that wants to wage real war on the left in the name of God and morality, but what they really want is power." He said with conviction.

"So, what's new Quin? These people are all around us."

I took a large sip of my beer and gave Quintero the look. It wasn't that I didn't believe him, it was just that I have become so accustomed to the pandering, the bickering, the lying, and the division that was overtaking our country that I felt it was just one more advertisement.

"Look at the viewing screen my friend." Quin said.

I looked up and I looked around the bar at all the viewing screens. Sure enough, all but one had some fashion of network news being telecast regarding a variety of politics, depending upon the conspiracy of the day.

"This country is in a state of chaos Bo and the networks are battling on who will believe what. They are battling against each other to form your opinion and take a side. The question is whose side will you take? Division is being sewn Bo."

I took a deep breath.

"Quin, broadcasts are not going to form my opinion! My opinion was formed a long time ago and those people that get opinions formed by watching viewing screens must be weak and easily convinced of anything. Besides, division is not BEING sewn, it HAS been sewn." I spoke.

"You are exactly right my friend! They live, listen, and convince each other of the way they want to believe. What you are not seeing is the effect this is having on our Nation. We are not a country of free thinkers anymore, my friend. You, me, and the guy sitting at the bar are all susceptible to being overtaken by this cancer of self-righteous thought. We must stop and see the big picture!"

I continued to gaze at the viewing screen.

"Quin, so what are saying? This so-called Freedom Manifesto is out to create a Jihad against the United States?" I asked.

"Not against the United States my friend, but within the United States. A Civil War is being planned. Not the North against the South but the Right against the Left and it's the big money and those that get the power that will win. They want this war. They are fueling these networks to stir the hearts and minds of the heartland to fight against each other. It will become a degraded society over which only a powerful few will rule. This is not a conspiracy theory Bo, this is happening." He said with the conviction of a political candidate.

I took a swig of beer and smiled at Quintero.

I wasn't sure what to think. Quintero had a way to stir up theory's and I felt I owed it to him to listen. I didn't think he was wrong. I just wasn't sure what it was he thought I could do about it. I finished my beer and ordered another.

"I'm going to have another but then I have to go." I said.

My beer came and we talked. I listened to him and found his sense of conviction admirable if not almost convincing. Quintero had heart. He was as honest and good as a man can come. If not for his short stature, he had movie star good looks with his dark hair and stylish clothing. I hope his heart leads him to the right place. I finished up my beer as Quin gave me one last thought.

"Where do you want to be in five years my friend?" Quin asked.

"I will have to give that some serious thought Quin. Now, I need to go and call Austin, he's in love." I prompted.

Not that I didn't enjoy Quintero's company but because I felt like I've heard enough conspiracy theory and philosophical meandering to find a change of scenery.

As I turned to leave, I glanced at the viewing screen and noticed that every screen was suddenly on the same topic. Everyone in the room seemed captivated by the monitor. This wasn't unusual anymore but apparently the stock market had suddenly plunged.

I looked at Quintero as he was smiling at me shaking his head.

"Coincidence Quintero! Coincidence!" I said as I walked away smiling.

I awoke to familiar surroundings in an unfamiliar state. I stood up and looked out the window to see several people walking off into the distance. The sun was beginning to set. I dragged the dead body of Mr. Thomas outside and left him a few hundred feet from the house. Unfortunately, dead bodies were becoming a common site just about everywhere. His burial would have to wait.

As the sun disappeared beyond the hill, I gazed around at what was once my home. I walked upstairs and climbed onto the roof so I could gain a good visual of the surrounding landscape. Dark filled the countryside. I looked up into the dark West Virginia sky to view the stars. Beautiful, I thought. Very peaceful. The night air was cool as I kept watch and drifted into thoughts from the past. The hours past. I kept a tight grip on my .365 magnum.

A distant scream disturbed my drifting thoughts as I pondered which way the sound was coming from. No telling. Perhaps from the East near the tree line but hard to tell. It was hard to get used to this kind of thing.

As the hours passed and dawn approached, I closed my eyes and drifted into a light sleep for what felt like a few minutes at a time. It felt so good to rest my eyes. Just get through the night, I thought. Daylight will bring a new day and hopefully closer to a new reality.

When the scream occurred once again the direction was unmistakable. East, I said to myself. The sun was beginning to peak over the horizon. I slowly climbed down from my perfect perch and began walking slowly toward where I heard the scream. I attempted to hide myself among the peach trees along the way that were once my favorite climbing trees with the sweetest fruit. Once upon a time I thought to myself.

The ground fog gave me cover as I approached what I assumed was the area of the sound. If not for the situation I would believe this to be a beautiful peaceful morning. I could even smell the scent of honeysuckle. I crept closer gripping my gun tight.

"Who be creeping up over there?!" I heard a deep male voice ask.

I froze in place.

"I've got an AR15 ready to let loose on you if you don't speak up!!" The voice said.

Through the early morning fog, I could only see a shadowy figure.

"My name is Bo Brown. I mean no harm. I thought I heard someone screaming and I thought I might be able to help." I hesitantly said.

As I slowly walked closer the fog gave way until I could see a middle-aged man with his weapon trained on me.

"Please, I don't want any trouble. I used to live in this area, and I thought I heard someone in trouble, that's all." I said.

"You just turn your ass around and go back where you came from before I blow twenty fucking holes through your ass, Homeboy!!" The man yelled.

I still had my gun raised and aimed at him. It was a standoff.

"If you put your gun down, I will lower mine." I offered.

"Homeboy, you'll get off one shot from that pee pistol before I riddle your ass and eat you for breakfast. Now I'm going to ..."

Before the man could finish his sentence, his head exploded from a heavy round as I watched his brains scatter and his body fall limp to the ground. I never fired a shot.

I dropped to the ground in defense with my hands pointing my .357 outward. I was trying to breathe but my adrenaline had kicked into the point of panic. What the hell was that? I thought to myself frightened of being next.

I scanned the misty landscape and made out a moving shadowy figure tied up against a tree in the distance. Suddenly another person ran to the tree. I got up and began to slowly walk over to get a clearer view.

I saw a man trying to untie a female from a large tree as he quickly removed a gag from her mouth. Once the gag was removed the lady screamed and cried hugging the man. I could only watch as the scene played out of an obvious rescue of some kind. The man turned and saw me approaching. He grabbed his weapon and pointed it in my direction. I raised my hands still holding my pistol.

"Wait! Please don't shoot!" I said.

"Who are you?" The man asked me.

"My name is Bo Brown. I used to live in this area, and I was investigating someone screaming. I mean no harm."

The man lowered his weapon which appeared to be a military assault rifle of some sort. I took a deep breath. The lady grabbed the man tight and held him in a long embrace crying. The man looked over at me while he held her. Both were war torn, dirty and anguished.

"I've been tracking this guy for a week." The man said.

"What's your name?" I asked.

"Danny" he said.

Danny looked over at the dead man.

"That man is Miguel Sanchez. He was a member of a gang that took my wife. I've been following him for a week. I'm not sure where the rest of his gang are but I'm sure they're not far. Thank you for distracting him so I could get a good shot at him. We need to get out of here." He said still fearful of the other gang members.

"My home is not far. You may both come with me."

I kept being hopeful that every time I saw this it would be the last time. It never is. The war destroyed the nation I once knew. It took my family, my friends, my desire to live life. I have thought to myself many times how such a thing could happen. Where were the balances of power? Where were the safeguards we were told about? Where was the safety net of democracy? These questions wore on me until they became unimportant anymore.

Chapter Two

<u>Austin's Wedding</u>

"First, I would like to say to my very dear and longtime friend, Austin, I love you buddy and I wish nothing but the best for you and lovely Francesca." I toasted on a beautiful summer evening in the New York Countryside.

"Now comes the hard part!" I added with a laugh and sip of my champagne.

I was very happy for the newlywed couple although Francesca was a couple months pregnant you really couldn't tell yet. The happy couple were hoping no one would notice as they were keeping the bun in the oven a secret for as long as possible.

Austin's Father Clyde Finch suddenly moved in to engage me in conversation.

"Hello Mr. Finch!" I said, greeting him as he smiled happily. He grasped my hand in a firm shake.

"Hi Bo, it's good to see you! I just wanted to thank you for that lovely toast." He stated.

"Thank you, Mr. Finch."

"How is you father?" He asked me.

"He's well, thank you. Both my mother and father are doing well, still at the old homestead in West Virginia. They'll never leave that place."

"West by God Virginia! Lovely place. What about you son, do you have a lady in waiting or are you content with living the single life?" Mr. Finch asked me.

"Uh, well sir I think I'm just content with the single life for now, but you never know."

"Remember to keep your moral compass pointing in the right direction son. Living without God and fornicating at a whim is not a good direction. Please heed these words."

Let me state that I never thought of myself as a wild fornicator nor a sinful person. Although I feel my spiritual guidance may be lacking in the God department, I took offense to Mr. Finch's words. In fact, I was more than offended, I was suddenly off balance and at a loss for words. This is rare for me.

I had met Mr. Finch only one time previously. I had reluctantly gone home with Austin on a college break several years back and was introduced to his dysfunctional upbringing. His father clinching his Bible as his mother cliched her glass of brandy as they attempted to convince me of their conservative views and why the unfortunate misguided "lower class" needed to learn to help themselves and be less reliant on Government resources while at the same time claiming it was Gods will that these people are so retched.

"Those kinds of people are sucking this Country dry", Mrs. Finch slurred. Mr. Finch would agree by quoting a verse from the Bible.

So, this brings me to this awkward occasion. The fateful son of these two wonderful conservative parents now marrying a lovely lady impregnated out of wedlock. I felt it was time I left this conversation. I excused myself with a smile.

It was a gorgeous day in the New York countryside as I slowly walked the grounds of the rented estate and looked out over the Hudson River. A fresh summer breeze blew from the East. My eye caught Austin and his lovely bride Francesca. They were all smiles as they walked toward me.

"Bo, thank you for being here!" Austin said to me.

Francesca gave me a welcome hug as they were both beaming with love and happiness.

"Bo, I saw you speaking with my father. I hope he was civil."

"Austin, he obviously doesn't know about you two expecting a baby!" I said.

"Uh, no." He replied.

Francesca lowered her head and smiled, then shrugged her shoulders as if to shrug off a nuisance and gazed at the river below.

"Your Moms not here?" I asked.

"No, no she's not." He replied.

"I'm sorry." I said.

"No need, and by the way please help yourself to the food and drink. It's plentiful and my dad is helping to pay for it!" He said with a smile.

"By the way Bo, see that gentleman standing over with my dad in the blue jacket?"

I looked toward a group of wedding revelers and saw a tall thin man, sharply dressed in a blue suit speaking with Austin's father.

"Yes" I replied.

"Stay away from him." Austin said.

"What?" I asked, puzzled.

"His name is Paul Blair. He's got money, he's political, and he's dangerous." Austin said.

"He's a friend of yours?" I asked.

"He's a friend of my dad's and came at the invitation of my dad to solicit interest and votes. Just typical of my dad to use my wedding day as a campaign boost for that new rising party. I can't stand it. Have you heard of the Republic Freedom Party of America?" Austin asked.

"I've heard of it but haven't given it much thought." I replied.

The tall well-dressed man began walking over to us. He had a smile and a swagger that insinuated his ego. I would guess his age to be late fifties with dark, well-groomed short hair.

I looked over my shoulder to watch Austin and Francesca walk away in quick fashion. I looked back at the man. I smiled at him as he reached out his hand to greet me.

"My name is Paul, Paul Blair." The gentleman said as he shook my hand with a tight grip. I had no choice at this point.

"Hello Mr. Blair, my name is Bo Brown." I replied greeting the man.

"Yes, I know Mr. Brown. May I call you Bo? Wonderful job you did as the best man. I think Austin and Francesca make a very fine couple and they seem so in love." He said.

"Yes sir, I believe they are." I said.

"They probably told you that I am in politics?" Mr. Blair asked with his eyebrow raised.

"They just briefly mentioned it." I said, of course, having just been informed by Austin of this man's purpose.

"I just want to give you something son and let you read it over. You seem like a bright young man Bo and there are a lot of decisions to be made and battles to be won in this country if it is going to get back on the right track again." Mr. Blair said as he handed me a pamphlet.

The man shook my hand and said, "God Bless you son" then turned and left me.

I watched as the tall man walked away in his confident swagger.

I looked over at Austin. He was smiling incessantly and pointing at me with chagrin. I looked down at the pamphlet I was just handed. "Let's bring back the good Ole Days" it read. "Get to know the Republic Freedom Party of America, THE next great Party, bringing people, values, and morality back together for a clear vision of our Country."

I folded the pamphlet in half and stuffed it in my pocket. I was ready for a drink and to continue with this celebration of love.

"My name is Danny Bennett. This is my wife, Brenda. We were traveling from Connecticut trying to get to Florida before Winter hits." The man said as he tended to his injured lady.

It was early September. Still warm days in West Virginia but it tends to cool in the evening. I used to love this time of year at home.

The use of vehicles or any other means of quick travel was gone as fuel was scarce. Walking is the only way. Gangs have commandeered most of the horses. With the coming of winter and the lack of electricity in most places for heat, many, many people were heading South. It was also rumored that US Army regiments had taken most of Florida and some other parts of the south back from the insurgent Freedom Party fighters.

"We were traveling with two families when the Delta gang or whatever the hell they call themselves came upon us. They killed a young teen for talking back to them and then killed his father for trying to defend his only son. They raped the women and then slit their throats. We attempted to escape but they caught my wife. There was nothing I could I do, but I managed to get away hoping I could live to fight another day and save her."

I looked around the house for anything of value. There was nothing here for me anymore. Gangs and others have scavenged it. The memories I once had of this happy home were long gone. I suddenly felt sick to my stomach. This was not uncommon in this life I was attempting to live. I wasn't living, I was surviving.

Brenda Bennett had the look of beaten, violated woman. She sat silently against the wall with a thousand-yard stare. Her dark brown graying hair lay matted and tangled with dirt stains. Her brown eyes had a look of desperation. It was obvious that she was probably attractive at one time. Brenda wanted to cry, however her dehydrated state wouldn't let any tears flow. I began to wonder as I watched her husband tending to her if she would not have been better off dead. Danny took a dry cloth and tried to wipe the dirt from her face.

"I'll go find water. I won't go far but if you hear a gunshot you need to hide. There's space under the stairs." I said.

There were no words that would help the situation. Comfort came in the form of needs such as water, food, shelter. My memories did not serve me anymore. Memories of good times, family, and love only to seem to hurt and create weakness in a time of desperation and fragile, misguided thoughts. I was alone. Alone with strangers I cannot trust. Trust: a word that had meaning once. A word that would bring comfort to knowing you knew someone. A comfortable feeling. That didn't exist anymore. I can't trust anybody.

I found water nearby from a flowing creek that my father had altered years ago to an irrigation channel to bring water to some of the cattle. I filled several large bottles, dispensed some iodine tablets for purification and made my way back home.

I sat against a wall looking ever intently through the window to keep watch. Danny continued to wipe his wife's face trying in vain to comfort her.

"I was a software engineer for a company in Hartford before the war. I left the company the day before terrorists bombed the building I worked in. Most of the people I worked with were killed." Danny said.

I took a sip of water and listened.

"I don't know how much longer we can do this. Brenda, honey are you ok?" Danny asked his wife as she sat staring into space. He continued to wipe the grime from her brow.

"Brenda, I love you. I'm so sorry. I'm so sorry, Honey." He said as he started to sob, holding her tight.

He looked up at me and took a sip of water and swallowed hard.

"I want to thank you for coming to her rescue."

"I wasn't coming to anybody's rescue Danny; I was simply checking out a situation. I did nothing."

"That's all it took. Distraction. You did enough. I have my wife back after following those animals for days. I want them all dead."

"I'm sorry what you and your wife went through." I replied, with nothing else I could say.

"So, who are you, Bo?"

I smiled and shrugged my shoulders as I took another swig of water.

"I wish I knew Danny. At this point I'm just a man caught up in a war-torn country with seemingly nowhere to go. Right now, I want to survive long enough to see what is left of this country. I'm not sure who's side you are on or if it even matters anymore, but we as a country need to get our shit together and reinstate our Constitution. I'm not sure if I'll live to see it. So much has been taken from so many and so many sacrifices."

Danny stood up and looked out the window. He ran his fingers through his wife's dirty hair.

"The war is over. I ain't on anybody's side. Most of the leaders of the Freedom State are all dead. What was once Congress is mostly gone, however I did hear there was movement to create a new Congress. I don't care. I don't even know what that means or who's backing them. What I do know is that we as a country are nothing more than a bunch of roving gangs raping and pillaging what's left. It won't happen to me or my beautiful wife again. They're still out there Bo. They're out there and they are coming for us. I'm tired my new friend, I'm very tired." Danny said with exhaustion.

He handed the water to his wife and smiled at her.

<u>Election Time</u>

"It is without hesitation, grievance, or latitude that I say that it is because of the fall from our core family values, a fall from our attentiveness to moral standards, and a fall from the belief in the almighty God that this perfect Union is no more!!" so stated Presidential candidate Stanley Brimley.

The crowd erupted into a roar in the large coliseum as the Presidential Candidate spoke his terms.

"I will bring back family values, prayer in schools, and so help me God bring this poor Godless Country to power once again!!" Stanley Brimley declared.

The crowd again erupted into cheers of thunderous clapping and yells of joy.

"We are the Freedom Party of America, and along with Gerald Hughes, we will represent truth, family values, strong morals, and of course military strength, by the order of God almighty!! Join my Freedom Party or forever be damned!!" the short but stately Mr. Brimley said as he finished to the roar of the crowd.

Stanley Brimley turned from the podium and began walking away only turning quickly to get another look, take in the cheers and wave to his supporters.

Paul Blair walked quickly to the candidate to help usher him out of the arena.

"Good job Stan! We've got 'em rallying behind you sir!" Paul Blair yelled to his Presidential Candidate.

The two men quickly made their way out of the arena and into a waiting large armor-plated Limousine.

"Praise Jesus! That gets my pecker up!" Candidate Brimley stated as he threw himself into the Limo.

"I can tell these fuckers anything!! I'm on fire! This country's going to be mine Paul! Mine! Mine to do any Goddamn thing I want!!" exclaimed the proud Stanley Brimley.

"Yes Sir but we need to make sure Mr. Hughes is on stage with you next time." Paul Blair stated as he was referring to Brimley's running mate.

The rally was over but the chanting in the arena continued. Stanley Brimley's Limo sped nonstop down the road.

"Turn the channel, Bo!" Olivia yelled from the kitchen as I looked for a dropped peanut under my butt.

"You know I can't stand that crap and that candidate is crazy!" Olivia said.

I clicked the remote and my 75-inch viewing screen fell silent.

"Honey, can I get you another beer?" Olivia asked.

I love the way her hair fell over her left eye. She would always give a quick toss of her head to quickly get the hair out of her eye. Olivia

Cane was quite a lady. I never thought I would fall in love, but she was the one. We met when I wasn't even looking. It was haphazardly and completely innocent. I was set up by Francesca on an evening that came at the end of a very bad day. I had fresh bruises from a car accident from that very morning. My car had been totaled, my arm broken, and I had a gruesome looking black eye. I was drowning myself at a local New York Pub when in walked Francesca alongside beautiful Olivia. This was the first time I noticed the way she tossed her hair back from her eye. I suppose Olivia felt sorry for me at the time or perhaps it was her caregiving instincts, but we completely hit it off; black eye, broken arm, and all.

"Yes! A beer would be wonderful my Dear!" I replied.

Her obviously beautiful blond hair, big brown eyes and cute figure totally enhanced her dutiful and bouncy spirit. She had an independence about her yet still seemed vulnerable enough to capture my male ego and instinct to protect.

"Have I told you Olivia that I met that guy Paul Blair at Austin and Francesca's wedding?"

"I've heard that name, who is he?" She replied.

"He's that moron campaign manager for Stanley Brimley." I said.

"Oh gross, those people are all crazy. You know they say and from what I've heard, Brimley's pick for VP is even worse than he is! A true nutcase dictator want a be!"

Olivia and I agree on most things, but something we both felt very passionate about is the distain of the Freedom Party of America. Since its rise and promotion of freedom for all in the name of religious rights and greed, this movement was becoming ever increasingly dangerous in our opinion.

"Bo, don't forget I have to work tonight." Olivia said.

I took a sip of my beer, threw a peanut shell in the trash, and turned off the viewing screen.

"I remember. Sorry Honey." I replied.

Olivia worked as a microbiologist at Harborview Memorial Hospital. She loves the lab but hates her job. The hospital keeps her overworked and underpaid. Because the turnover is so high the hospital is lacking in trained skilled lab techs like Olivia. She feels abused.

"It sucks for me, but I'll get through it." She said.

"I know you will. You always do. By the way, I've been meaning to call my mom and Dad. I'm still trying to talk them out of voting for Brimley next week." I said.

"Oh good!" Olivia said, "What do they see in him?"

"Olivia it's the same old thing we keep hearing. It's all about CHANGE! They hear the word freedom and fall for this guy's rhetoric! I can't stand it!!" I replied.

I took a last swig of beer and sat back watching Olivia gathering her items to take to work. It drew me into a hypnotic state that was quickly dashed by the sounds of the street below. I stood to look out the window of our small old New York City apartment. From the third story window, I could hear the chatter and hustle and bustle of the outside world. Election day was next week. I kept wondering what was to become of our country. "It's a shame." I thought to myself. "What is this world coming too?"

Once Olivia had departed for work, I picked up the phone to call home. The anticipation of the conversation with Mom and Dad was evident, however I was now at a point where I couldn't, nor do I care to talk about politics with them. As with most in this contentious election season arguing politics with my parents is not worth it. My parents were retired, living on a large West Virginia farm enjoying the rolling hills of peach trees and peace. Our views on life were very different. I grabbed the phone and made the call.

"The fly fishing has been good down on the creek this week Bo, I wish you were here!" Dad said.

"That's great Dad, I wish I were too." I replied.

I found myself falling into this conversation routinely. Validating the fact that I love them yet finding myself taking them for granted for the years of raising me.

"Your mothers been a little under the weather this week so she's lying down resting in the other room."

"Well Dad, don't disturb her, let her rest, just let her know that I love her."

Throughout the conversation I never mentioned the elephant in the room. Neither one of us did. The election. I grew up being taught that divided we fall and united we stand. This country had become so divided. Something I haven't felt or seen before. Something that was looming over the country like a wet smelly blanket. I felt a change coming. I see something in the eyes of people on the street. It seemed to be nothing I could explain or understand. These times were not like the turbulent 60's of years ago. There is no rioting, only limited uproar from the populous. Nothing that anybody but the politicians could seem to put a finger on. It seems as if the country was waiting and wanting something to happen.

Change. I kept thinking of that word. I suppose my old friend Quintero Rodriquez was right. The Freedom Manifesto was the groundwork for the Freedom Party. It was all about power and money. Something that I suppose the populous knows little about. The manipulation of the masses through false media reports to gain power and influence. The people wanted change. Something I learned from my mother, be careful what you ask for.

Chapter Three

<u>The Calvary Arrives</u>

"I've gathered what I could, so it's time we get out of here." I said to Danny and Brenda as they awoke from a decent night's sleep. It was already late morning, so we needed to get moving.

Despite the gangs and scavengers coming through, my old home still maintained some of its old qualities. Curtains my mother had hung, a scratch on a wall that I remember my father put there when moving in the new refrigerator, even an old comforter laying in a heap on the floor from my childhood. The views haven't changed but the memories were distant.

"We need to find food and I'll fill the canteens with water." I said.

Brenda began to speak last night but only softly and only to Danny. She's traumatized by the brutality that she experienced as a rape and beating victim. She's lucky to be alive and even luckier to be back with the man that loves her.

As we made our way down the old dirt road, I looked back at what was once my home. Such distant memories. Now, with one weapon tucked in a holster and another strapped around my shoulder I realize it was a different life.

The late morning gave way to early afternoon as we walked along a long, lonely road. It was unusual not to see people traveling along this route south this time of year.

Suddenly we heard rapid gunshots in the distance.

"It's coming from that direction!" Danny yelled as he pointed North.

"Ok, well we are heading South. Let's get out of here."

"We need to move a little faster Bo; I don't want that gang behind us to see us." Danny said.

We picked up the pace as the sound of the gunfire grew closer.

"That's a lot of automatic weaponry!" I said as the rapid pop, pop, pop sound rang through the countryside.

Suddenly I saw dust on the horizon coming up over the hill in front of us. I quickly yelled for Danny and Brenda to take cover. We fell in behind some fallen logs in a gully on the edge of the road.

"Quiet" I demanded.

The sound of several horses coming down the road grew louder as we tried to melt into the ground to hide.

Brenda started to quietly moan and began to sob incessantly.

"Danny, you've got to quiet her down!" I demanded.

"She's scared Bo!"

I looked Brenda in the eyes as I came close to whisper to her.

"Brenda, I know you're scared, I'm scared as well. We are all scared and we all want out of this. The only way to get out of this is to get out of here. Please try to calm down and let these men go by." I whispered.

She couldn't look at me. Her head lowered as she continued whimpering. She was broken. She had no will left in her to fight. This once beautiful young lady was completely spent.

The horses came ever closer as we could now see their hooves as we peered through the underbrush. They slowed as they approached. They were so close now we could hear the horse's breath and snort. The men on horseback didn't speak. I held my breath.

Suddenly the silence was broken.

"Virginia National Guard! You are surrounded. You will raise your hands slowly, stand up slowly or be shot." A man yelled out to us.

Suddenly two men on horseback flanked us and approached quickly from the rear.

"Do as your told or be shot! We mean you know harm!" The man yelled out again.

We looked at each other, raised our hands in unison, and slowly rose to our knees to obey the man's commands.

We could still hear gunfire in the distance but getting closer. The heavy cover from the leaves of the forest gave shelter from the late afternoon sun, almost causing darkness.

"Harrison, confiscate their weapons and get them to a safe place." The man in charge said.

A rugged looking man, I assume was named Harrison quickly gathered our weapons as another man quickly zip tied our wrists. Both men were dressed in military fatigues with heavy armor. Several troops on horseback followed the man in charge as they quickly rode toward the gunfire. Harrison and another man led us further into the woods behind a large boulder.

Brenda was sobbing uncontrollably as the men sat us down behind the rock.

"Your National Guard?" I asked the young man.

"Yes Sir. Please keep the woman quiet. Were you all running from the gang?" Harrison asked.

Danny attempted to calm Brenda as he leaned over and kissed her on the cheek.

"Her name is Brenda, and she's been through a lot." Danny said to the soldier.

He then leaned over to whisper in her ear.

"It's going to be alright Honey. I don't think they are here to hurt us. Calm down baby." He quietly said in her ear.

"What's going on? Who are you guys?" Where did you get the horses? I asked Harrison.

"Who the hell are you?" He replied as he pointed his gun at me.

"My name is Bo Brown. We are just travelers heading south for the winter. Trying to get to Florida. Brenda has been through a lot. That's her husband Danny. We rescued her from a rogue gang not too far back." I said.

We suddenly heard loud explosions in the distance and more rapid gunfire. There was obviously a battle going on.

"What's going on Harrison?" I asked the soldier as he looked toward the explosions.

"We are here to eradicate the Delta Gang."

"The Delta Gang?" I asked in total ignorance.

Harrison looked at me and smiled.

"Well, I'm assuming you obviously aren't with the Delta Gang."

"We are just travelers!"

"Hold tight sir and everything should be sorted out shortly."

The explosions and gunfire began to subside. Harrison waved toward the road as we sat helpless against a rock with our hands still bound. Danny did all he could to continue to comfort Brenda.

Brenda looked up at me from her slouched position.

"You the man that saved me?" Brenda asked me, now suddenly less distraught and has obviously decided to talk to me. I smiled at her.

"I suppose I helped, but your husband saved you."

"Thank you."

Harrison walked a few yards away to wave down a couple of his soldiers riding in on horseback. The sounds of the horse's hooves thumping the ground grew closer.

"Gather those people up and bring them over." A commanding voice bellowed.

Harrison ran back with his gun over his shoulder and began helping each one of us to stand up.

"Come with me."

We stood along the road now in view of smoke about a mile and half back from where we came. The commanding officer maneuvered his horse directly in front of us. He stared each one of us down with a tough dirt laden grimace on his face.

"Sir these people claim they are travelers heading south. They appeared unaware of the gang location or motive." Harrison advised.

"Is that right?" the Commander asked.

We stood still. Not knowing what to do at this point or who's side they were on.

"Who are you, where are you coming from and where are you going?" the Commander asked.

"Did you kill those bastards?!" Brenda yelled at the tough military man on horseback.

The tough Commander looked over at her.

"I hope you killed every one of those sons a bitches!" She yelled at the Commander again.

The Commander paused and repositioned his large horse closer to us.

"I'll ask again. Who are you? Where are you coming from and where are you going?" The Commander had a controlling but demanding tone. I noticed he kept one hand on his sidearm.

"Sir my name is Bo Brown. My homestead is North of here. I came across these people, Brenda, and Danny yesterday as they were fleeing the gang. We took refuge in my old home for the night. We are now on our way south to Florida, trying to get there before winter." I explained.

"He helped save me!" Brenda belted out.

The Commander backed his horse slowly away and turned.

"Sergeant Harrison, get these people some fresh water and a ration. We will set up camp on the hill over there." The Commander instructed.

He then stopped and turned his horse back toward us.

"We will release you, however I would not recommend you leave the safety of our unit. Please get some water, some food, and some rest. We will talk in the morning." The Commander stated to us as he galloped his horse away.

We took the Commanders advice, and we were happy we did. Sergeant Harrison became a confidant and important ally over the next 4 days. The Delta Gang, it turned out, were very bad and desperate people. Commander Bell, as I came to know him and his troops all but wiped out the Delta Gang during the brief battle. It was discovered that it was the Delta Gang that had captured Brenda. Unknown to the three of us they were only moments away from attacking us when the troops arrived.

The National Guard troops that we were now imbedded numbered forty men and six women. Commander Bell was formally in the navy but joined this group of soldiers when his battalion went either rogue or were wiped out. They were well trained, armed, had connections and more importantly, had horses, food, and drinkable water. They had been fighting for almost a year. Unbeknownst to most people, when the fighting broke out many of the men and women in the armed services had already been divided along political and religious lines due to heavy propaganda, infighting, and persuasion from both sides. Rogue militias began dividing off from the regular corps. It became a civil war in the worst way. There were no geographical dividing lines, only philosophical and moral lines that soon grew into a fight for survival with the creation of many rogue gangs. Troops attacked and brought down the electrical grids. Armies thought in unison that taking the grids offline would give an advantage to themselves only finding out that they had disabled and crippled an entire country and turning the clock back on society a thousand years. The comfort of being with a formal fighting group was a relief. Hope could be seen in the eyes of some of the soldiers as they spoke of a new nation. For the first time in a long time, I could feel things changing for the better.

Assassination

Olivia and I watched our television screen as President Stanley Brimley were escorted from the White House into his large limo and disappeared inside. The country was in turmoil with the stock market crashing, a recession wreaking havoc, and American Civil Liberties disappearing. In only three short years we felt the country was at the brink of a disaster.

So, Olivia and I sat on the couch together in our New York apartment and watched the havoc unfold on the news. Twenty-four hours a day the news seemed to replay the division and turmoil that was occurring at an alarming rate within our country. The chaos of the country was becoming increasingly the norm. News channels were replacing network series as the most watched screen viewing. Apparently, the country was entranced by the division of the country and the turmoil broadcasting live on the news every moment of every day. People couldn't get enough.

I heard a commotion coming from the street below. I walked over to see what was going on and cracked the window to listen. It was a well-dressed man confronting a lady holding a sign on the corner. The sign read, JESUS LIVES, SEEK REPENTENCE!!

"You cannot force me to believe like you!" A man yelled at the woman.

"This country is full of people who don't know Jesus Christ and rebel against Jesus Christ through their sins. We are standing up for Christ and against EVIL DOERS!"

A companion to the woman walked up with another sign that read, LGBT — LET GOD BURN THEM ALL! and began railing against "Sodomites."

"Hey Olivia, come look at this!"

We both looked out upon the show below.

"President Brimley! President Brimley! He is finally here to bring salvation back to this country!" The lady yelled.

Several automobiles began honking their horns in support of the signage.

"This President has become some kind of savior or prophet to these people." I said to Olivia.

"Oh Bo, what is happening?" Olivia quietly asked.

We continued watching the circus unfold below our window.

"This has to STOP!!" The man yelled.

"Try and stop me!" The lady holding the sign yelled back.

"You don't understand! This new guy is bringing about a decline in the international order! The standing of the office of the presidency is in jeopardy, and there is an erosion of democratic norms!" The man yelled.

"You need to see the light of JESUS!!" The woman yelled back.

"What has Jesus done to help this country? What does our government have to do with GOD? GOD has forgotten us!" The man yelled.

"NO!" The lady yelled. "My child over there is Gods answer! Love, life, goodness and beauty rests in the eyes, the heart, and the innocence of the young." She explained as she pointed to a young girl.

Suddenly and unexpectedly the man pulled a handgun from his jacket pocket and began firing upon the woman. The woman backed away and fell with her sign flying off into the street. The man continued to fire two more shots into her companion. Another sign fell to the ground as the companion fell against the building smearing blood along the wall.

"You have your wish!! You are now going to see your GOD!!" The man yelled.

As Olivia and I watched in horror it only got worse. The young girl, no more than five, came running up to the lady and began calling out to her mother.

"Mommy? Mommy? WAKE UP!"

Police ran in from across the street as the man stood with his firearm now down by his side seemingly crying.

With no warning one of the police officers put his pistol against the man's head and fired one round through his temple. The man's head jolted to one side as bodily fluid ejected from the opposite side of his skull. The child began screaming as the other officer grabbed her by the arm and attempted to pick her up. Both Olivia and I turned away in horror.

Three people lie in blood beneath our apartment window. Olivia began to scream and cry. I was in shock as I took Olivia into my arms to try to comfort her. It had seemed in an instant that the world had gone mad.

I was on my third beer when Olivia awoke from her nap. Our day off had taken a dramatic turn at the site of the horrific incident we had witnessed hours earlier.

"Hey K, are you doing ok?"

"I couldn't sleep."

She reached into the refrigerator for a bottle of wine.

"The world is crazy."

I looked out the window to see the mess below being cleaned up.

"Bo, that cop just shot that man at point blank!"

I looked at the grievance and pain on her face.

"The cops are now judge and jury with no consequences! You break the law and POW your dead!" She said, understandably upset.

"I see more and more shootings and death at work and now right outside my own WINDOW!"

"I want out of here Bo. I'm not sure how much longer I can take this."

We sat and held each other. Neither saying a word or a sound except the occasional sip from our wine or beer glass.

I broke the silence. "Should I turn on the news?" I asked.

"NO!"

After about an hour of drinking, helping us come to terms, along with the help of some old classic music, we seem to have come to grips with the event of the day. I hesitantly turned on the screen to view some news. There was no mention of the catastrophic event that occurred under our window at all. The incident was just that. Another random act that has seemingly got caught up and drowned out by all the other bad things going on in the world and around us.

Upon awakening the next morning, it felt as if my eyes had to be pried open. I rolled over to see that Olivia had already left for the hospital and it was not even 6:00 AM yet. I climbed in the shower to begin my day.

Times were tough at Harcroft & Harrison Consultants. Rumors have been circulating for about a month that the company was going under. It was confirmed on this day. We were all told to pack our offices and leave. It was 4:00 PM in the afternoon and the company had the balls to get a day's work out of us before telling us we were out of a job. Bastards!

I went to find Austin and found him at his desk sitting quietly at his desk.

"You ok buddy?"

"I don't know Bo. I guess so. I guess we saw this coming huh?"

"I suppose so."

I hadn't mentioned the incident the day before to Austin. The world was getting crazy. I didn't want to unload any more bad news on my friend. I tried to let it go. Besides, now we had a whole different set of issues to deal with.

"A Lot of people get laid off Austin. We will be fine!" I said, trying to make light of the situation.

Austin just looked at me with a grin.

We both walked out of the building together and separated to go our ways.

"See ya later Austin."

"Ok Bo, take it easy." It was the last time I ever saw Austin.

Waking in the morning with Olivia is a delight in my life. Often, she's already gone to work so in the mornings, on the occasions she's beside me, it is always a treat. I remember it was a crisp cool morning. The apartment window was open only so slightly to keep the noise out but let the fresh air in. I took a deep breath as I rubbed my eyes. Olivia made a gentle moaning sound. I left the bed to let her sleep and went to have my morning cup of coffee. I turned on the viewing screen to the local news as I made my way around the kitchen. The news on most days was of some sort of tragedy or another. This morning was a bit different as I could deduce by the announcer's tone.

"Again, we repeat, President Brimley has been assassinated. It is confirmed that he passed around 1:10 PM London time. That would be 8:10 AM Eastern Time here in the United States. Again, only a few minutes ago in London England during the Peace Summit the President of the United States was brutally shot in the head and assassinated. From what we understand the assassination was carried out by Secretary of State Alvin Tyler. We will have more information as it becomes available, but the entire incident was caught on video as the president was giving a speech in front of some of the members of Parliament and Prime Minister Sheffield."

"Wow! Olivia! Olivia!"

I ran into the bedroom.

Olivia rolled over sleepy-eyed and looked at me.

"The President has been assassinated!" I yelled.

"What?" she abruptly asked.

"He was just assassinated in England! It's on the tv now!" I said in my dire excitement.

I quickly walked back out to the living room and sat in front of the tv shortly joined by Olivia still trying to wake. We listened to the broadcaster.

"Again, we are sorry to bring you this news this morning. President Brimley has been assassinated. It is confirmed that he passed around 1:10 PM London time. According to official reports we are hearing he was shot in the head by the Secretary of State Alvin Tyler. Alvin Tyler was on tour with the President and was known to be an associate to the President. This comes as a shock to us all."

"Oh my God! Our own Secretary of State shot him?" I asked out loud.

Olivia sat saying nothing. The rest of the morning we watched the accounts of how Alvin Tyler apparently accompanied the president to the stage and shot him in the head. He was immediately tackled by General Sean Bishop of the U.S. Army. Tyler attempted to escape however General Bishop wrestled him to the ground. There was a scuffle for Tyler's gun when General Bishop reached to his own sidearm and shot Tyler in the chest, killing him.

That evening we watched as Vice President Gerald Hughes was sworn in to become the new President of the United States. Hughes had control of the Freedom Party and now had control of the country. Olivia and I felt our country was being torn apart by ignorant, self-absorbed, racist, and partisan nonsense. Nobody liked to see the President shot and killed and we surely did not condone the act, but it was with eager anticipation to see where the country would go from here. Who was Gerald Hughes?

Twenty-three days past before anyone in the country heard a word from our newly appointed President Gerald Hughes. He had not been seen by the public since his swearing in. He was not seen at the Presidents funeral, nor has he had a press conference to offer condolences and comfort to the American people. It was all so odd. We felt as if the country was losing grip of itself with very little information to go on. The press corps had been shut down and finally, on December 24th, the new President came on viewing screens across the country to make an announcement. Olivia was working at the hospital as I watched the address by myself on a cold blustery Christmas Eve in New York City.

"I'm appearing before you this evening to encourage prayer and peace on the eve before the Christ's birth. First, let us pray."

The President recited a prayer naming Jesus as the Lord and Savior to comfort all in these horrible times and to give rise to the righteous and calling for the evil to find damnation. The President continued with a few words only ending the address that puzzled many.

"There will come an event that will purge the many and leave the few! I leave you with these words and ask that if you have not repented, NOW is the time to do so! GODBLESS!"

I watched as the President walked from the podium and shook hands with several people standing off to the side. He was stoic and stood tall. Something felt very out of place as a feeling of uneasiness came over me.

Soldiering

"It's going to get worse before it gets better." Sergeant Harrison shouted out to a group of soldiers awaiting orders. Sergeant Harrison was a young but rugged man. He was a soldier's soldier and battle worn. He became important to us and those close to him called him Sarge.

"Alright here's the plan! We want to arrive in Charleston by May 25th. We will parallel old Interstate 95 along the eastern seaboard and eradicate gangs that are setting up tolls and extorting from those that are heading south. We, my gang of good merry men and women are the hope for these people seeking refuge! There are many people heading south. Once we are in Charleston there will possibly be another objective. There has been talk of a military ship in Charleston harbor that is still in working order. If that is the case, it will be our job to seize that ship and use it to our advantage. Once we are at that point Commander Bell is to meet with Colonel Hatcher for further instructions. That is the plan and those are our orders! If you have any concerns or questions, please feel free to come see me."

I watched Sergeant Harrison walk away with purpose and confidence. I paused in my thoughts when something he said stuck in my ear. I looked over at Danny.

"Danny, who is General Bishop? I asked.

Danny looked over and replied, "You don't know who Bishop is?" He asked me as if I should know. I knew the name sounded familiar.

"Bo, he killed Alvin Tyler the Secretary of State that killed President Brimley!"

"On my God! I knew I've heard that name before!"

"He was imprisoned by the Hughes regime shortly after the assassination. Alvin Tyler was conspiring with Hughes to kill the President and General Bishop discovered this shortly after during his investigation of killing Tyler."

Sargent Harrison overheard and spoke up, "He's a good man, and he's determined to create a new America. His escape from the Hughes Regime is legendary. Mr. Brown, you've been living in a world of death, destruction and chaos trying to survive in a dark world. You are with us now. These soldiers and a few more divisions out there are what is left of a civilized world. It's time that the death, destruction, and chaos is turned around and put on those that continue to wreak havoc, bring disorder, and thrive off the pain of others. It is now their turn to suffer. We will succeed Mr. Brown and we will bring this country together again."

The Sargent walked away. I looked over and saw Commander Bell on his tall horse watching so eloquently and stoically over his troops. I couldn't help but think I was in a very historical moment and what our founding fathers must have thought and went through to create a free and once strong nation.

"Danny, we're going to fight with these men." I said feeling positive about our future for the first time in a long time. "And I want to know everything about Bishop and his great escape."

"Yea, he killed Brimley but that's what started this whole mess." Danny said with a smirk on his face.

As night fell, we pushed toward Charleston, I couldn't help but reflect on where I've been and where we may be headed. I raised my canteen to my lips and took a sip of water as I stared into the campfire. I sat up and gently brushed some dirt off my pants as I suddenly took notice of someone. Like most soldiers the dirty gentleman was wearing his standard issue camo. It was apparent the fighting and stress of war had taken a toll on the man. He was sitting directly across from me with the light of the fire gently giving way to the features of his face. His face was dirty, but I knew that face.

"Quintero? Quintero is that you?"

The man sat motionless as his eyes met mine.

"Quintero, it's Bo!"

The man slowly sat up straight.

"Bo? Oh my God Bo?" he asked as he suddenly realized it was his old friend from New York.

I stood and walked around the small campfire and presented myself.

"My old friend Bo! How are you, my friend?" He asked.

I grabbed his hand and pulled him in for a hug. I hadn't seen Quintero in years.

"I can't believe it's you Quin! Are you ...with these troops? How did you end up with the Virginia National Guard?" I asked.

"I am. Not officially of course, but I joined them about a year ago when the war broke out. They call themselves the Virginia National Guard. It's a ragtag group from all over but mostly from Virginia. What about you? What are you doing here? Have you joined the fight?" He asked.

"It's been very hard Quin. Your troops found us a few weeks ago as I was leaving home. A gang was after us." I said.

"Us? Who is us and what are you talking about?" He asked.

"I'm traveling with a married couple. Danny and his wife Brenda are in a refugee tent. We are all preparing for the journey tomorrow. Brenda was abducted by the Delta Gang, and I just happened to come across them on my old property in West Virginia. To make a long story short I was at the right place at the right time. Your band of brothers and sisters found us."

"That was you! Yes, I heard the story. We took out that gang!" He stated.

"I thank you for that. Quin, I can't believe it's you!"

I looked at Quin with astonishment when we came across each other. The once radical guy that I used to meet for happy hour was now soldiering in a war right beside me. I smiled at him as I thought of all our past days.

"...and I can't believe it's you my old friend." Quin replied.

"I'm sorry about Olivia. I can still remember your beautiful wedding."

I smiled at that thought as it seemed so long ago. Another life.

"I have to leave you now my friend, I am on watch." Quin rose and dusted the dirt off his khakis.

"We will catch up more later, go get some rest." Quin said.

"I will Quin. Damn good to see you crazy man!" I said as I strode toward my tent.

The hauntings from those in my past were constant. I continue to see Olivia with her beautiful hair covering her left eye as if she did it on purpose to drive me crazy. Her gentle toss of her head to remove the hair from her eye. Her upbeat laugh and beaming personality. Damn I miss her.

Dawn came early. I was up before light packing up the rations and standard issue gear that Harrison had found for me. The camo fatigues were worn but it offered me the comfort of being among the soldiers. I awoke having the feeling of belonging. Strangers such as Danny and Brenda were now friends and comrades. My old friend Quintero was now beside me and giving me a sense of belonging once again.

As I walked to fill my canteens, I saw Quintero riding high upon a proud looking steed. In his left hand, he held a rein with another horse galloping along beside.

"For you, my friend!" He said.

I broke into a large smile.

"Quin! Really? A horse for me?"

"You will ride beside me my friend as comrades. We will fight together!" he said proudly.

I looked at the large horse with excitement as well as hesitation.

"Uh, Quin, I..."

"Get on your horse Bo!" He yelled.

I grabbed the rein as the horse looked at me waiting for control.

"Get on your horse Bo!" Quin repeated.

I patted the side of the horse's jowl as his large brown eyes attempted to anticipate my next move.

"These horses are war horse's Bo. You must mount him quickly and take control. Do you want him or not?" He asked in anticipation.

"Quin, I, I..."

"I'll give you five seconds to get on that horse soldier!" A booming voice said as I turned and saw the Commander and his horse standing behind me.

"Does he have a name?" I asked.

"Lightning!" Quin replied. I shouldn't have asked.

I took a tight hold of the rein as I placed my foot in the stirrup and pulled myself up and into the saddle. I held the reins tight as Lightening thankfully cooperated with my every move. I was not necessarily a total stranger to horse riding, but it did come as a surprise and rather an abrupt chance to hone my skills once again.

"Mr. Brown, I have heard good things about you from Mr. Rodriguez. I hope to see good things as well. The horse is yours if you agree to soldier and carry orders." The Commander said.

"Yes Sir! I'll do my best Sir!" I said.

"Have your friends load your gear in the truck. You're one of us now Mr. Brown!"

The road to the interstate was about a two-hour gallop with Quintero and a few other Calvary Soldiers. I left Danny and Brenda behind knowing they were in good company with Harrison and several other troops. Riding through the Virginia mist was like going back in time. The peace, the cool breeze, I even thought I smelled the scent of honey suckle. The peace and distant thoughts quickly escaped me when we suddenly heard gunshots.

"Hold up!" Quin stated as he raised his right fist to signal stop.

We circled and I could not make out where the shots were fired from. We scanned the landscape.

A sudden shot rang out as one of our men was hit in the side. Quin quickly raised his weapon and rang out a barrage of gunfire into the underbrush ahead. He then drove his horse directly at the threat. I was impressed and at the same time frightened by what had just occurred.

The threat was neutralized as a single dead young man no more than fourteen years of age was pulled from the underbrush. Large bullet holes riddled his body.

"What a waste." Quin said.

"It saddens me that these boys are brainwashed into working as scouts for these gangs. They either fight us and die or go back to the gang and die because of being coward. Just a waste." Quin stated as he looked at the dead boy.

"In any event they know we're here now. We must move on and prepare ourselves for a possible battle. How is Shafer?" Quin asked, looking over to the man that was wounded.

"Shafer was shot in the side, and it went clean through Sir! He needs medical attention." A trooper said.

Quin barked out an order. "Grimes take Shafer back! Shafer, you better live to soldier on Son! The rest of you let's move on! Eye's open!"

I glanced down at the young dead boy. I had become hardened by the sight of death. It was a world without mercy.

It was less than prophetic that I had to learn a new way of life. I was not just trying to survive anymore. My life had turned from survival to a life with purpose. Compartmentalization and dividing my life into segments were now routine. Killing, seeing young dead bodies yet having the compassion to hug a friend around a campfire seemed bizarre. To be a soldier is to be one that serves for a purpose. The purpose, I suppose, was to bring a good life to those that follow us. We soldiered on.

Chapter Four

<u>Contentment</u>

I find contentment to be fluid and diverse. A multitude of things can bring one contentment. Contentment in a job, contentment in a friendship, even contentment with your favorite vehicle, however, contentment in love is something we search for perhaps our whole life. Contentment in love can be as elusive as catching a butterfly by its wings in midflight. I found something elusive about Olivia. From the way she tossed her hair to the way she softly smiled at me after a bad day, Olivia had whatever that rare feeling of a bond, friendship and connection was. Love I suppose.

It wasn't long after the assassination of President Brimley that I wanted to bring peace and order to my own life and the one I love; forever. The country seemed to be in a chaotic state but that didn't mean that our lives couldn't be rich and fulfilled with order brought about by our own happiness and contentment.

So, on a beautiful Spring evening, I asked Olivia to marry me. Her reaction was twofold.

"What took you so long!?" and "Of course, Yes!!" She excitedly replied with her wonderful beaming smile.

"I'd like a small wedding." I said, only to be interrupted.

"I want a big wedding!" she exclaimed to my surprise.

I held her in my arms smiling from ear to ear.

"I only said small wedding because I thought that is what you would want!" I said.

We both laughed and took in the moment. And with that, contentment was found in our lives as we smiled and gazed at each other in a happy snapshot of time.

I called my best friend Austin and broke the good news. He and Francesca seem to have an on again and off again relationship and at this very moment it appeared to be off again. I reassured him relationships take work, and he needs to take the time to listen and practice patience and to grow the relationship. Austin was not the patient type.

With the loss of my job, Olivia and I were content with a small wedding. The Country seemed to become more and more divided as each day passed. Witnessing the killing in the street below our apartment shook us to the core and we conceded to moving out of the city into a small house in Greenwich Connecticut from a little savings I had. The craziness was all around us and it was hard to escape. The fact that Olivia and I were struggling in an uncertain world gave us a sense of fatigue that was beginning to consume us both. We were crazy in love yet felt the cloud of an uncertain future.

What was to happen next would shatter our world forever.

What I really enjoy about sunrises is the fact that they have always represented new beginnings to me. The dawn of a new day just seems to bring a sense of wonder and hope to what the day will bring. It is surprising to me that so many take mornings for granted. One beautiful morning I was lying in bed next to Olivia with the new sunrise beginning to bring soft new daylight through the bedroom window when I asked Olivia a simple question.

"Good morning beautiful, how about a walk this morning before you go to work?"

She slowly rolled her head, so her eyes met mine.

"I would love that, Bo."

As we strolled on a cool but not cold morning, I can remember something different about that walk. We didn't discuss politics, we didn't discuss money, we didn't discuss problems, we simply had no discussion at all but rather fun banter back and forth about the flowerpots and the color of window dressings people chose on their various homes. It was a delightful sense of belonging we felt with one another. Meaningless chatter along with a quick quip and a light laugh or giggle to step by.

"You are my Sunshine!" I said to her with a smile.

"And you are mine" she replied.

When I kissed Olivia goodbye that morning, I had forgotten to mention to her that I was planning a special meal that evening. My cooking skills had increased with each day I was unemployed; something Olivia would benefit from although we both knew my time could be spent in a much more valuable way if only, I could come across employment.

My day continued like any other crazy day in America on that day. I didn't feel I could trust all news reports anymore. The honest news journalist was being ostracized by the makeshift government and the new President Gerald Hughes. It felt as if the country were waiting for something better to happen, a new election, a new face for America, someone with hope and a positive message. It wasn't there. The country was torn. I was living in a bomb casing waiting to explode. I quickly made my way to the small market down the street that still carried well-stocked shelves.

I was slowly making my way through the bread section when I heard a woman scream. I looked over to her. She was standing looking at her phone furiously pacing. I ran to her and asked what the matter was. She was sobbing incessantly.

"We are under attack! I just had a call from my husband, and he stated we are under attack!"

Her muttering wasn't clear, and she made no sense to me.

"Under attack from who?" I asked.

Suddenly I saw several people hurriedly running out of the store. Then someone yelled, "A militia force associated with Hughes Regime is attacking our area!"

I was stunned and confused. People began to run from the store grabbing items as they went as chaos ensued. I couldn't believe what I was seeing.

"We must leave!" the lady said to me, still sobbing. I dropped my shopping agenda and quickly left the store. Most people were quickly leaving as I was but several continued to loot as if it was the end of the world. What was I witnessing?

I ran to my car as I saw smoke rising from the downtown Greenwich area. Then suddenly I heard the wale of sirens coming from all directions. Then, it suddenly occurred to me that Olivia was downtown at the hospital. I quickly put a call into Olivia trying desperately to reach her with no success. I hurriedly got to my car when I heard a loud shrilling sound of a rocket whistling overhead and a large explosion and boom only 200 yards from me. I was frantic and desperate to reach Olivia. The panic in the streets ensued and it prevented me from going anywhere. Olivia was not answering her phone. As smoke drifted through the air and people ran through the streets, I inched my car closer to a small road to find a way back home. I realized there was no way to get to the hospital and therefore no way to get to Olivia. I was going to have to be content with attempting to continue to reach Olivia by phone. As I turned behind a large box store building attempting to flee the area, I could see what appeared to be military tanks through the trees on the road adjacent to me. "My God!" I thought to myself. I picked up speed and found my way to a road leading toward my house. My hands began to tremble as I gripped the steering wheel as hard as I could. Suddenly my phone rang, and I quickly looked at the caller ID. It was Olivia. I quickly veered to the shoulder and pulled over so as not to get distracted by the other terrified drivers and sounds of distant gunfire.

"Olivia?"

"Oh my God Bo, where are you?" She asked.

"Olivia I am trying to get home. I am pulled over off Hamilton Avenue. Are you ok?"

Olivia couldn't speak as she began to cough uncontrollably.

"Olivia?"

I could only listen to her struggle to form words.

"Bo, we've had an emergency message from the CDC indicating chemical weapons being used against Americans." Olivia struggled to say.

Olivia's voice was weak as she continued to attempt to speak as she coughed.

"I don't know the full extent of what is happening Bo, but I love you!" She said.

"Olivia! Olivia!" I called out.

"Olivia, can you make it home?" I asked.

"Olivia I can't get to you right now due to military vehicles and blocked roads. Can you make it home?" I asked again.

I heard nothing on the other end as the phone fell silent. I attempted to call her back several times to no avail. I was angry. I put the vehicle in drive and stepped on the gas as hard as I could to find my way to the hospital. As I approached an intersection I watched before me a large military vehicle with mounted automatic guns that began firing into the line of cars and people in the intersection as if they were simply shooting beer cans. Large caliber bullets ripped vehicles and people to shreds as they took command of the intersection. As the gun began to turn my way, I quickly turned into a side road and attempted to flee the dire situation. My mind was racing. My heart was pounding as I tried to look down each street for a thorough fair. All was blocked by military and chaotic scenes from hell. Chaos was raining down on America.

Twenty-eight days past since the takeover of the Eastern United States. The regime led by President Hughes took over a large faction of the military by dividing Congress and then assassinating members that did not become loyal. It was a quick and ugly campaign that rained down like fire in hell. The Pentagon became dysfunctional, and State Governments fell to the wayside as Hughes and his so-called Freedom Party now ruled what was left. Our once strong allies now abandoned us and viewed us as a weak Banana Republic. The world economy faltered.

I learned of my beloved Olivia's assassination when the hospital was taken over by the regime. I never said goodbye and sobbed for a solid week. I wanted to believe it wasn't true, but reality didn't exist any longer. Contentment no longer had meaning. I sat lost in a dark world hearing only the cries of the anguished and the protests of the desperate.

The Freedom Manifesto was the groundwork for the Freedom Party. As my friend Quin once warned me, "Be wary of the those that seek control in the name of freedom." Freedom is a word that can be thrown around for the good of anything. In the case of the Freedom Party, they used the word to conjure those seeking the same malignant causes to align a rebellious faction of racist, hate filled tyrants that believed righteousness is the cause and effect from power and greed. The dangerous yet genius part of the Manifesto was the alignment with the wealthy, powerful and the religious. This was to assure their sustainability. Hughes played his part by becoming the leader of the Party and arranging for President Brimley's assassination. In any event, democracy is fragile. In the end, it was democracy and the promise of those freedoms and beliefs that imploded among those that sought it and believed in it the most.

Following the coup and destruction it brought, the Freedom Regime which came to be known as the Hughes Regime, attacked, and killed all of those that resisted. Battles and unrest waged across the United States but somehow Hughes held onto power.

Chapter Five

<u>Charleston S.C.</u>

It was late Spring a year following my Olivia's death. I was now part of the Virginia National Guard. We continued to parallel Interstate 95 South until we reached Highway 78 into North Charleston. We were an exhausted group along with our horses and we now had limited supply chains. Sergeant Harrison was excellent at communicating our orders and we soon became friends. As we traversed the landscape scarred by two years of battle, I was glad to be in the company of such men.

Commander Bell summoned us for brief gathering before we were to make our assault upon Charleston. I paused and thought to myself; like something from the first Civil War sitting upon a hill just outside of the Southern City of Charleston, I likened myself to an old Calvary soldier on the brink of battle. We have had many skirmishes with rebel forces, gangs, and marauders but nothing of what was about to face us.

"Men, I want to thank all of you for the hard-fought journey we have taken. Before us lies our prize. We will divide up into three squads. Harrison, Johnson, and Beck will lead the squads. Harrison, you take the first squad forward and head on. The other two will attack from each side of town and flank. Our objective is to reach the Warship Dreadnaught on the Cooper River. We have intelligence that leads us to believe that this ship is fully functional and capable of capture. The ship sits at the end of a long terminal at an abandoned oil refinery. Your leaders will give you more details. Once on the ship we tend to sail it to Florida and help develop and defend our new Government. Key West and South Florida is the seat and stronghold of our new leadership ladies and gentlemen! Our end goal is to take back America!" The Commander ordered.

I gazed at the men around me. Quin looked over and gave me a smile and a nod. This was the feeling I had been seeking. The need to be part of something bigger than myself. It was a great feeling. Thank you, Virginia National Guard.

I watched the fire light flicker and could smell the scent of Army rations cooking as I awaited my turn with a plate. Quin had mentioned to me that another small rebel force from the North would be joining in on the fight that was to begin at dawn tomorrow. I was given a ration of what had become known to the soldiers as "Quicksand". A mixture of breakfast cereal, powdered reconstituted milk, and crushed peanut butter crackers served warm. On this night we were given a small piece of cooked beef from a local butchered bull. It was a special night in anticipation of tomorrow's raid. I walked over to quin and sat beside him on a log with my precious meal of "quicksand" and steak.

"Do you know anything about this group that will be fighting with us tomorrow?"

Quin dipped a piece of bread in his quicksand and took a bite. I'm not sure where the bread came from, but I was now assuming it may be for the higher ranked soldiers. He smiled at me.

"They're coming from some of the same areas up North we are from. It will be good to improve our numbers." Quin stated.

I agreed as I enjoyed chewing my piece of meat and anticipated what tomorrow would bring.

"I am told there is electricity in South Florida." Quin said.

"Really?"

"Yes, many of the regimes' loyalists fled to South Florida in the early days of the war. Our government collaborated with Cuba to defend the peninsula in exchange for the lifting of all sanctions in the Communist State. Can you believe that?" Quin stated.

"I had no idea, Quin. So, we are now friends with Cuba?" I asked.

"Sort of; there is a man by the name of Mateo Garcia who was the Mayor of Naples. He collaborated with a few Congressmen that foresaw what was happening with the Freedom Party coup and arranged a backdoor to preserve our former government or at least what it represented. You know, the land of the free and brave apple pie stuff. Many of the military commanders and their troops that did not go along with the coup fled to Florida and eventually set up a quasi-U.S. Government that is as close as we get to what we had. I am told there are other leaders spread over the Country that know of this and are fighting their way to get there. We will take back our country Bo."

I finished my meal as I absorbed what Quin was telling me. I thought of my mother and father and what they would think of all of this had they survived. They were simple people who enjoyed the pleasures of family, peace, and a good work ethic. My Dad hated politicians and Mom followed his lead. I can remember him saying, "Good leaders surround themselves with good people. There are few good people in Washington."

Why they voted for Brimley is beyond me. I suppose you just don't see things coming. I must admit, growing up I didn't take much credence in politics. I did enjoy history and especially loved American history and took pride in being an American. I don't know what history will unfold or be told about these times. I do know that my pride in being with this group has become unwavering.

I thanked Quin for the information, I found it profoundly encouraging. I spent the rest of the evening by myself looking at the sunset in the west. I watched the soft breeze gently blow a leaf in a circular pattern as if expressing its excitement for nightfall. The gentle sounds of men talking through their anguish behind the sounds of birds heading to roost. I found myself nervously ready for battle as I lay my head down. "Madness", I whispered to myself.

I was awoken by the sounds of footsteps outside my tent.

"Mr. Brown?" I heard a voice whisper.

I raised my head to see Brenda peeking into my tent.

"Brenda?"

"Yes Sir, it's me. I'm sorry to wake to you but I just wanted to wish you luck today." Brenda said.

Dawn was just breaking over the hill and the birds were flying about excited for the day as the sound of the song was telling.

"Thank you, Brenda. Are you ok?"

"I am. Danny will be joining the raid, but I will be staying behind. We decided it was best. I will follow behind and join you on the ship to Florida." She said with a smile.

"Thank you, Brenda. I will watch after him."

I sat up and readied myself as I rubbed the sleep from my eyes as I awakened myself from a nervous night of unrest. "Let's do this." I said to myself.

"Bo! You're with me!", Quin said as he quickly walked toward me and grabbed my arm. "Bo, we are going to be briefed by Sergeant Harrison."

We joined a small group of men surrounded by strong calvary horses as Sergeant Harrison began to speak.

"Men, we will be leading the way on horseback through the ridge beyond that hill and come out near an old high school. We have strong surveillance that there may be defensive positions of the enemy near the school. Gentlemen, we are the point. We looked upon Harrison as our leader, a father figure. The man was probably no older than twenty-seven or twenty-eight but a man among men. He was large with the biceps of a weightlifter and the dark skin of a fisherman. When he walked among you his presence was known and the group looked up to him and accepted him as a fine leader.

"Our goal is to make a path for others to follow. Johnson and Becks men will be flanking on each side of us to create trap for the enemy as they try to retreat. We will fight and move any enemy forces into the firing line of these two groups. Johnson will flank from the North and

Beck will flank from the south. We will meet approximately one-half mile from Dreadnought and then collaborate and attack together to take her by force if we must. Any questions?" he asked.

I had no questions at that point. It was go time.

I grabbed the reins of my sturdy war horse Lightening, threw myself upon him and settled in the saddle. Quin had his game face on and gave me a thumbs up. We gently tapped our horses and began heading east into Charleston. Before we could get out of camp a young man stopped me and handed me four hand grenades and an extra round of ammo for my rifle. I acknowledged him by tipping my hat and putting the loot into my side saddle. I then gently patted my horse for a slow gallop to catch up with the others. I found myself concentrating on the task at hand but at the same time gazed upon the evergreen trees that lined the road. Abandoned cars, a child's bicycle, a stray dog, and an older couple looking and waving at us as if we were in a holiday parade. Such a strange yet familiar setting.

We paralleled Highway 78 heading toward the Cooper River for several miles before coming upon our first threat. It was man of very slight build standing in the middle of the highway holding a sign. We slowed our pace as we approached carefully. It's almost as if we could hear the rumbling of activity in the distance but could not see anything.

Sarge raised his fist to give the all stop signal. "Williamson, approach the subject slowly and see what this is about." Sergeant Harrison ordered. Williamson slowly made his way forward toward the subject in the road holding the sign. The sign read, "The Kingdom of God is Upon You!" Suddenly the man threw down the sign and ran quickly away. Williamson halted his horse as we watched the frail man hide among some brush near a building and disappear. Sarge then raised his hand to move us forward again slowly. We were quiet and focused on the task at hand to seemingly stay alive. As we gained some ground without incident Sergeant Harrison spoke. "Let's pick up the pace men. I can smell the river."

As we approached the high school my grip on the reins became tight and I found myself sweating profusely in the late May sun. Sarge stopped us near an abandoned warehouse. We aligned the horses behind a wall and gathered for the assault on the high school. The horses would remain here to be picked up later, while we made the rest of the way on foot. I said my quick goodbye to Lightening.

Harrison divided us into three groups. There was a total of twenty-one of us. His group of seven would go first up the middle. I was with Lieutenant Beck's group flanking on the left and a man by the name of Rick Johnson led his seven men flanking on the right. Quin was with Harrison as they started to move in. We moved in slowly and choreographed our movements, attempting to conceal as much as possible between abandoned homes and trees. I stepped lightly behind a fellow soldier named Ben Sampson. I briefly looked to my right to see if I could find Quin when all hell broke loose. The sound of whizzing bullets filled the air with loud snaps and popping noises as the bullets hit our surroundings. The fog of battle descended upon us as I had no idea where the fire was coming from. I was following closely behind Ben when I witnessed a perfectly clean shot explode his head and brain matter. I fell behind a small tree and looked towards Ben. He could not be saved. The bullet fragments and whizzing went on around me. I could see the others firing upon the onslaught and watched as I saw Sergeant Harrison run without hesitation toward cover near a large tree by an open school window. I dashed forward following the lead as Harrison tossed a hand grenade through the window. I closed my eyes and fell against a tree. A large explosion rocked the area. The bullets were still coming as I began firing toward the windows of the school. I could now see rifle barrels of our enemies as they fought to save their lives as we were fighting to save ours. I suddenly became hyper aware of my surroundings. It was as if I could see from above and I had an overwhelming feeling that today was not my day to die. I watched as Harrison pointed me to the right side of the building and I looked and focused on one of our wounded. I had no fear as I ran about twenty-five yards toward my comrade. Somehow, I made it through the hail of gunfire, grabbed the soldier by his gun belt and dragged him to nearby cover. It was Quin. He had been shot twice in his left arm, once through his shoulder and once through his leg. I did the best I could to relieve the bleeding, he was still conscious.

"How are you doing my old friend?" I asked him as the battle continued around us.

"I'm hurting buddy", he replied.

"Quin, I think you are going to be alright. These wounds don't look too bad and you're breathing and talking. I will get you out of here."

Quin gave me a smile then suddenly grimaced and gave a groan.

"I know buddy. Your gunna be ok!" I said.

I then looked over to the Sarge as he was motioning for us to advance. I fired a few more rounds through the windows as I noticed the return fire starting to lighten up.

"Quin were moving into the school. You will be fine here until I come back to get you."

"Ok Bo, thank you. I'll make it. Sorry I'm out of the hunt. Go get 'em Buddy." Quin replied.

At this point our plan was working as Sarge was heading to the front entrance of the school with Lieutenant Beck on the right side and myself and Rick Johnson heading in from the left. Both Johnson and I crawled into broken out windows simultaneously firing and striking the enemy down before they got a shot off. We found ourselves in what appeared to be an old science classroom long since its last true use. We both crouched low as we made our way along opposite sides of the room with the anticipation of meeting at the doorway. An enemy combatant quickly appeared in the doorway attempting to fire upon us as we both landed accurate and fatal shots at his body. The room was smoky with the smell of gunpowder and cement dust. Johnson then made a move out the door quickly looking left then right. It was suddenly quiet except for a few rounds going off by Lieutenant Beck's group down the hallway. We had the enemy on the run.

"Quin has been hit! I need to go retrieve him." I exclaimed to Johnson.

He nodded affirmatively. I made my way through the left entrance of the school and ran back to Quin. As I approached, I was fired upon, and a bullet slightly grazed my left forearm. I heard several shots coming from the school as my comrades took out the sniper.

I had tied two makeshift tourniquets around the severe wounds Quin had suffered and they appeared to be working. He was still conscious and able to converse. I grabbed him around his shoulder as he winced in pain and helped him to his feet. One of my comrades then showed up and we carried Quin to the school.

"I guess I owe you a beer for this." Quin joked as we propped him softly against a wall in a classroom that now became our resting spot for the next few hours.

"I think you owe me two." I replied.

"Men, we will rest up for two hours and continue through Charleston. We are not out of this storm yet." Sergeant Harrison said.

"How are you doing Quin?" The Sergeant asked.

"I can make it Sarge."

"Good! I expect we can be at the boat by morning." The Sergeant replied.

Chapter Six

<u>**Devotion**</u>

Once the war started, I realized that my life up and until that point was a life of privilege. I never had wanted for anything as I grew up with a good life on a West Virginia farm with good parenting and a good education. My struggles and stressors revolved around my love life, school, work, and what I thought at the time was my uncertain future. Of course, I never could imagine exactly how uncertain my future would become.

Spiritual devotion was important to my parents. They were not necessarily religious however they held a certain regard for God and the Christian beliefs. I respected that. My mother would read the Nativity Story from Mathew every Christmas. I saw it as a joy and a tradition. My family, though spiritual, didn't see the benefits of belonging to an organized religion or church.

My Spiritual devotion as I saw it during that time was quite less. I didn't find myself thinking too deeply regarding any afterlife or heavenly presence. I knew the difference between right and wrong and attempted to treat others as my parents had always told me.

"Treat those well as you would like to be treated." Seemed like common sense to me. I didn't engage in criminal activity, nor did I need to. I didn't engage in drug activity other than the occasional beer every now and then and I have always felt like I was a pretty good guy, or at least as good or better than the next guy. I suppose that proves some arrogance and prejudice, but I tend to believe that arrogance and prejudice are not necessarily forgivable by a higher power. Perhaps we should find it in ourselves to forgive each other and ourselves if the need arises.

I had friends tell me I was going to hell, and I've had friends tell me I was surely bound for heaven. I suppose that is not their decision either way and I'm not real sure what difference it really makes, especially while living on this earth, we all do the best we can.

I guess I have too many questions regarding devotion, spirituality and religion and I don't count on, nor do I seek anyone to answer those questions for me. I find my sense of devotion of a spiritual kind to be highly personal. I believe my beautiful Olivia felt the same way. We would sometimes have these discussions and I found them profound and fun with her. She was my person that I could talk to about anything. She was amazing and once I found out she was killed I took a fresh look at my life and our beliefs. I suppose she now knows. She knows if there is a heaven, for, I know if there is, it is the only place she would be.

When Quin came to me and warned of an imploding democracy, I had a very hard time accepting it and believing it. A Democracy, so I thought, was made up of shared values with tolerance to allow others to believe in what they wanted and to not impede those you did not agree with. That is the way it has been for over 200 years in the United States of America, or so I thought.

When I met Paul Blair at Austin and Francesca's wedding it was a foretelling of the trouble to come. The pamphlet that the man had given me was not only a clear sign but looking back I wonder why I had not taken more action.

"Get to know the Republic Freedom Party of America, THE next great Party, bringing people, values, and morality back together for a clear vision of our Country."

In just those few words I can now see such disregard for others and blatant discrimination that it makes my skin crawl. What people? Who's values and morality? And who's clear vision? I soon discovered it was not mine, but many Americans bought into it.

When the Republic Freedom Party of America; now known as the Freedom Party Regime took over, I was caught off guard. My inability to see what was in front of me, what Quin had warned me about was about to collapse my world.

The Freedom Party assassinated my beautiful Olivia. As with many others, the world became a very dark place.

So that brings me back to devotion. What is it and why would I care or devote myself to anything at this point? It was something that I believe haunted many during this dark time. All I know is that while sitting against a cold wall of what once was a school in a Country called America in a city called Charleston, exhausted from a firefight against people that I once considered my fellow Americans, I had to find something in me to carry on. I looked across the classroom and above the dry erase board were the words, Go Rebels! I couldn't help but think about the irony.

My eyes were just closing when I heard Sergeant's voice. "Time to move Ladies and Gentlemen, break time is over!"

Sergeant Harrison began a briefing as we gathered ourselves together and stood up.

"Johnson's soldiers to the North are encountering heavy fighting as they attempt to make their way through the 841st Transportation Battalion or what once was. It is the only thing between them and the Dreadnought. Our enemy has taken possession of many weapons that were once part of battalion and Army Reserve Center there. We are going to make our way to Virginia Avenue and head North to flank the enemy from the south and join our soldiers in the fight."

We left the school and headed in an easterly direction toward Virginia Avenue. Quin stayed back with a medic at the school, and he was told he would be catching up with us soon. A wounded man would only slow us down. About thirty minutes later, with no resistance, we made it to Virginia Avenue where we turned North. We could hear the fighting in the distance only a mile or so away. I could smell the brackish water of Cooper River, so I knew we were close.

We approached the overpass of the Mark Clark Expressway. We had been warned of snipers on the overpass, but Sarge pushed ahead anyway. "Shortest route." He said. The bombed out remains of the bridge which expanded across the Cooper River were now in ruins and mostly underwater except for a portion on the east side. My curious mind started to wonder how a ship would make it through the submerged rubble. I suppose I needed to start to worry about the present and I gazed ahead.

Within fifty yards of the overpass our luck ran out, shots rang out and the first thing I saw was a clean shot to the head of a soldier about ten feet away from me. He dropped to the ground. We broke into two groups as we ran to cover among the rubble of several bombed-out oil storage tanks on the side of the road and a park with a boat landing on the other. The automatic fire was heavy, and they had the advantage of higher ground on the overpass. We began shouting at each other as confusion reigned. I was pinned against a tree near the boat landing. Our cover was light, and I could see we were taking casualties. This was going to be a long fight as our group was now separated. I could hear the Sergeant yelling, but I could not make out his words. Automatic fire continued to hit against the oak tree that was saving my life. I could smell the scent of fresh wood, gun powder and oil. War is very strange.

Time appeared to slow down as I huddled against that oak tree. We attempted to return fire but the advantage our enemy had on us was too much. Their automatic weapon fire seemed endless. I saw Sergeant Harrison yell something and make a motion with his arm when a bullet hit his hand and he grasped it in pain. His attempted communication was lost on me. I could hear the enemy on the overpass yelling and communicating with each other and what seemingly sounded like laughter through their gunfire. Suddenly the gunfire stopped. I was frozen against the tree amid the strange scents and smoke in the air. It was quiet for a moment until Jimmy Conroy attempted to peak around the large oil tank he was hidden behind. A sniper took advantage and laid Jimmy to rest with a direct shot to his throat. "Damn!" I said to myself out loud. I knew that boy just turned twenty.

For the next two hours we remained pinned in our places awaiting instruction. Those two hours gave me plenty of time to think about things. I knew our goal was to be at the Dreadnought by first light. It was now late afternoon. Nightfall may bring us an opportunity. The laughter and partying of the enemy on the overpass continued. I had little to no contact with the Sarge, so I had no way of knowing any plans. I wondered what became of Johnson's group just to the North. Were they still in a firefight of overwhelming odds or did they get through? I had no way of knowing as I sat against the tree in my protective cover.

Nightfall came when suddenly the gunfire started up again. What was odd is that the enemy was firing at someone else. I gained the courage and peaked beyond my cover. What I saw was amazing! It must have been Beck's group!

"Sarge, I think it's Beck's group!" I yelled across to others. As the firefight raged above the overpass, we were able to scramble out of our cover and run under the bridge to the other side of the overpass. It was Beck's group!

"The calvary has arrived!" Beck yelled at us. "What the hell are you all doing down there?"

As the enemy scrambled with many casualties a few attempted to climb by rope from the overpass. We quickly took them out from our vantage point.

"No prisoners!" Sarge yelled.

The fight lasted a long fifteen minutes when the sounds of guns stopped. Only the moaning of the dying enemy remained. I thought about Quin and looked forward to seeing him again. It felt like a low point and a high point at the same time.

We hugged our saviors. Beck and his men had intel of our situation and came up to flank from the west. It was successful for those of us that lived. For Jimmy Conroy and the gentleman shot in the head and many of our enemy it was not. We all took the rest of the late night to rest under the overpass. I hoped to never be back at this place again. I hoped that whatever beliefs and devotions those dead men had were enough to sustain them through the pain and the afterlife. My hopes fell silent as I closed my eyes to forget the day.

Chapter Seven

The Dreadnought

I've always loved the sounds of birds in the morning. They sounded particularly sweet this morning. I awoke to their sweet sound that seemed to drift along the soft breeze that made no mention of the chaos that surrounded me. The hue of the morning light was just beginning as I had lived through another night and ready to take on another day. The Dreadnought was only 15 minutes away on foot. Sarge got us up and we began to move out. A few of the enemy were still laying on the ground where they fell wearing the insignia of the so called "Freedom Fighters" on their jackets, an American Flag embossed with the Cross of Christ. As I walked, I thought about the sacrifices they were making for their "Freedom". They took up a fight against their fellow Americans as they feel their own set of beliefs or doctrines were important enough to kill over. "Freedom", as it has become to be known, is apparently defined differently by those that choose to integrate the word into their own belief structure. Freedom, as it is known by me, and those I choose to fight with is a word that should have the same meaning for all.

We met no resistance that beautiful Spring morning. As we walked east, I soon saw the Dreadnought come into view. She was an older vessel but still held her beauty. She was an old 509.5-foot, Arleigh Burke Class guided missile warship. She originally would complement a crew of 380 U.S Navy Sailors. The U.S. Navy is now splintered along with all the services. On this day, smiles and laughter broke out among the ranks as we came upon her.

"Well, would you look at that!" Stan McKinley said in his Irish accent. As he put his arm across my shoulder he asked with a smile, "Looks as if we are taking a cruise, aye?" I smiled back at him and said, "Aye Stan! What a museum piece!".

Several men on horseback suddenly came up from the rear and trotted alongside of us. It was Lieutenant Johnson and his men that had just arrived from the north. A couple of the men on horseback trotted alongside of us. "We heard you had a scuffle last night!"

"We did." I replied to a man riding high on a proud horse. His cowboy hat shaded his eyes from the late morning sun.

"Looks like quite a prize ahead!" The man said as he gazed at the Dreadnaught.

"I would say so! I hope we have the crew to get us out of here." I replied.

"We do! The ship was taken two days ago by Colonel Ivan Hatcher and his men. There were 26 of them but he lost 7 in the fighting. I heard they beat a small division of Freedom Fighters that were protecting it. Luckily for us several of the original crew are still on board maintaining the ship, including Captain Surles. They're on our side. The missile launchers are no longer operative, but it's got a 5-inch 62 caliber turreted deck gun that should be able to inflict some serious mayhem!"

"What's your name my friend?" I asked.

"Tobey Longstreet! I'm from just outside Austin Texas. I ran a small horse farm and now I like killing insurrectionists! Yes, I said insurrectionists! I don't call them Freedom Fighters because there not! We are the true Freedom Fighters! Those people are insurrectionists against the true founding of democracy and what this country originally stood for." Tobey stated defiantly.

"Nice to meet you Tobey, my name is Bo Brown. You seem to be a wealth of knowledge Tobey; how do you know all this stuff?"

"Stick with me my new found friend, I will open your world!" Tobey said as he lightly kicked his horse to gallop off. He turned as he galloped away and tipped his cowboy hat at me. "Nice to meet you, Bo!"

We were now dockside and gathered with the Sarge for a briefing before boarding. Gunshots could be heard in the distance as the sun was getting high in the sky.

"Alright, listen up men!" Sarge yelled out. "I am proud of all of you for your dedication to the fight and for each of you finding your way here to the Dreadnaught! You will board and we will be deporting within one hour from now. Find your bunk, get some rest, and get ready to fight another day. I will see you on board!"

I marched along the gangway making my way aboard the ship. A young man no more than sixteen years old waved at me from the deck. Upon closer inspection the Dreadnaught was a tired worn girl. A "rust bucket" I heard one of the men say. She felt alive as I stepped upon her deck. The vibrations and hum of the generators made her feel as if she was ready as ever. Her worn and rusted bolts may have said otherwise. "Welcome aboard!" an older gentleman stated as each of us made our way. I must admit, I have never been aboard a warship. When I made my way to my bunk room as I was greeted by a familiar face in a cowboy hat. "Mr. Brown, is it?" He asked. "Yes sir, and your name is Tobey if my memory serves me." Tobey reached out his hand to shake mine. "Looks like we will be bunking mate's buddy!" He said. I smiled back at him and shook his hand. "Where's your horse Tobey?"

"Buddy let me tell you something! That ain't no horse! Tabasco is a warhorse! That horse has saved my life on several occasions, and he is my family. Unfortunately, Tabasco will not be making the voyage. He'll be alright. He's been through a lot worse than this. Maybe he can find a filly to lay in the hay with tonight. Something I wish for all of us right now!" He said with a smile. "Speakin' of layin' in the hay, I got to get me some shut eye. I'll take the top bunk." He climbs into the top bunk and tips his hat to cover his eyes. "Goodnight, Gentlemen!"

The small cabin had a musty odor with two bunk berths on each side. The berths were small and covered with the appropriate sheets and a blanket. A small pillow for your head. The ship was a classic naval grey in color with no extraordinary furnishings other than your typical military props. Signage indicating exits along with warnings of different types dotted the passageways and various compartments. As with most ships I have ever been on, which is very few, the passageways consisted of what appeared to be a maze of different corridors and compartments. The hum and vibration made the ship feel alive. The smell had a hint of must and diesel. I lay myself down in the small berth and tried to think of happier times. Damn I missed Olivia. I stared at the berth above me and began to become annoyed at the snoring of Tobey. Apparently, my new friend had some serious sleep apnea. On this occasion I chose to ignore it and I quickly fell asleep.

My sleep was short lived when I was awoken by a loud knock on the wall next to my berth. "Brown!" I heard a loud voice yell. "Brown wake up! Sergeant Harrison wants to see you!" The man yelled. I quickly responded and came to my senses. "Follow me." The man said. I found myself in what appeared to be a larger stateroom that had been converted into a meeting center. Sarge had a seat at one end of a small oblong table. "Have a seat Mr. Brown." As I took a seat, I noticed what looked to be a list of names in front of the sarge. "As you know Mr. Brown this ship is very short crewed. We need to make every effort to utilize each man as efficiently as possible. I know you are not military, but you have wartime and battle experience. I appreciate your service and what you have contributed so far. You've done a good job. I am officially enlisting you as a service member with the rank of Private First Class. Congratulations, I will be assigning you along with Tobey Longstreet to man the deck gun. Tobey is a fantastic Calvary Officer; he will apprentice you in the operation of that gun. Any questions?" "No Sergeant and thank you Sergeant, I look forward to serving anyway I can." I replied. I exited the room with a smile on my face. This was the first time in a long time I felt good about something. I was now officially a soldier. A soldier with a duty. I felt a sense of pride come over me as I rarely have felt. Sergeant Harrison had a way about him that made you feel good about what you were fighting for and gave you a purpose for that fight. I knew the purpose. As I walked the corridor back to my cabin, I came upon a sign that read **Mess Hall**. I turned to my left and made my way as I felt the sway of the ship now moving. We were underway. I entered the mess hall and suddenly I saw a face I recognized.

"Brenda?" Brenda looked at me with delight and a smile.

"Oh my gosh! How are you, Bo? I just knew you had to be on this ship!" She said.

"How did you get here?" I asked perplexed. "They asked for volunteers soon after you left so Danny and I volunteered to follow in a large group hoping to make it Florida! I told them I can cook, and Danny can fight and clean." I smiled intently at Brenda, knowing the journey she had been on and knowing what she and Danny had been through. "It's so good to see you!" I said with a smile. Brenda's eyes glanced behind me. "Look who I found." She said. I looked back and saw Danny walking up behind me. "Bo!" Danny said with a large smile. He grabbed me and we hugged each other tightly. "Damn good to see you man!" He said. "I'm glad to see you both!" I said.

Pleasantries were exchanged and a few tears and laughs were had as we caught up with each other on our journey to the ship. I grabbed myself a fresh cup of coffee which I had not seen, smelled, nor tasted in at least a year. I shook hands with the two men working the mess hall and they were very happy to accommodate the crew with the rations they had on hand. They handed me a bowel of cooked yellow rice topped with a small piece of chicken and black beans. This was more than I had ever expected or had in my belly in quite some time. So far, I have been enjoying this cruise.

A very strong vibration woke me from a deep needed sleep. I arose out of my bunk and gazed over at Tobey as he was still snoring away in his own deep sleep. Suddenly the sound of a very loud siren went off throughout the ship interrupted by "Battle Stations! Battle Stations!"

Tobey rose quickly and looked at me. "Time to go to the gun Bo!" he exclaimed. "Quick! Let's move buddy!" He stated as he slipped into some boots that lay on the floor in front of him. I grabbed my nearest shirt and pants and flung on my boots. This was all new to me so I thought I would follow Tobey's lead. "Oh, hell son! Which way to that Dag gum gun!" He yelled as we exited our cabin. We could barely think or communicate with the loud siren and announcements blaring throughout. "This way Tobey!" I yelled as I turned and began retracing my steps. It was to our disadvantage that we had yet to have a drill. Time hasn't allowed it since we were recovering from our last battle. There were 52 men and women aboard this vessel, and all appeared to be scrambling around confused like. We made or way down the corridor and up a ladder. I knew we were close. I looked up a stairway and saw daylight coming through the hatchway. "This way Tobey!" I yelled again as he followed quickly behind me. As we reached the deck two men ran toward us and yelled, "Follow us!" We made our way to the impressive 62 caliber turreted deck gun. Rapid fire automatic guns began blaring all around the ship as the crew began firing at the enemy. It was now apparent that the enemy was approaching in several boats attempting to blast their way aboard the Dreadnaught. We had somehow made our way around the downed Arthur Ravenel Jr. Bridge and made our way around historic Ft. Sumter. It was quite ironic. The two men quickly accessed the gun and began the loading and firing process. Tobey directed the men, "Blast those damn boats out of the water!" The gun quickly turned on its turret and took aim at a fast-approaching boat with approximately 8 men firing toward us. Tobey simply pointed at me, pointed at a large 55-pound projectile, and then pointed at one of the men. I grabbed the projectile and lifted in from its cradle and handed it off to the man. The man quickly loaded the gun and with the loud order of "Fire!" the other man pushed a button and the large gun fired into the boat as it approached. The boat disappeared in a large blast and fireball. As I attempted to recover from the blast of the gun I only slightly heard "Reload!" as my ears were ringing from the concussion of the blast. Boats appeared from all directions. Again, Tobey conducted his pointing ritual without saying a word and I again began lifting the projectile to the man. Once again, the orchestrated firing went off destroying yet another enemy boat. I learned to cover my ears and duck behind an iron plated cover as the ritual continued for several more rounds. The mighty Dreadnaught was now out of Charleston Harbor and in the open Atlantic as the swells of the ocean became apparent on deck. Gunfire subsided as Tobey and the two men looked back to see the damage they had inflicted. "Yeehaww! Hot damn!!" Tobey yelled as he grinned at us. "Just another day in paradise boys!" He yelled.

My ears were ringing as the sirens ceased. I couldn't hear much of anything but only looked upon the smoking remains in Charleston Harbor. I looked at Tobey and grinned. "You're a crazy Texan aren't you Tobey?" I asked with a smile. "I am sir!" "But ain't that who you want beside you in a fight?" He asked back. "Yes sir, I guess it is!" I replied. "By the way, consider yourself apprenticed!" I didn't hear him, so I asked him to repeat. "Consider yourself apprenticed!" Tobey yelled in my ear as we laughed it off.

Soon after the fight we mustered for a briefing from Captain Surles alongside the sarge. "We lost a few men today. I'm saddened by that fact, but this was only a skirmish, and I am proud of the fight you took to them. There will be more so prepare yourself. If you don't have a good firearm, please report to the armory, and get one. Your useless firing a handgun at approaching enemy boats or ships. We are an army. Let's behave as one. Good job today, that is all, you are all dismissed." The captain said.

I watched the sunset that evening from the deck of the Dreadnaught. I needed the time to reassess the last few days and contemplate what was coming. I knew Quin was in sickbay and I owed him a visit. The salty air and the sound of the sea was comforting. I closed my eyes and sat quietly against the steel of the ship.

We made it through another night. The Dreadnaught sliced through the ocean as I looked up upon a beautiful sunrise.

"Well hello mate!" Stan McKinley said as he greeted me. I was still sitting slumped against the ship on deck as he checked on me.

"Decided to sleep in the salty sea air last night did ya?" Stan asked with his thick Irish tongue.

"I guess I did." I said, still waking up in humid salty air.

"The sarge found you up here after a brief search since you didn't show up in your bunk." Stan said. "He decided to leave you here to sleep. No harm, no foul."

"Where are we Stan?" I asked.

"We be a little past Port Canaveral Florida. Time to get up and get on my watch. These waters could be a wee bit dangerous for us."

Stan grabbed my hand and helped me to my feet. I briefly surveyed the seascape. The water was a deep blue with no land in sight. We knew we were headed south by the angle of the sun.

"Let's get the day on, shall we Laddie?"

I smiled at Stan and shook my head in the affirmative fashion.

"Stan, I need to stop by the infirmary to check on a buddy of mine." I said.

"Aye, I understand your Mate Quin is fine. He's got a few bullet holes in him, but they patched him up rather well. Follow me, but we need to make it quick." Stan said. We made our way through the ship's interior, and I followed Stan down a long corridor. The one thing that kept mesmerizing me was the ships' lighting and electricity produced by the generators. It's several years since I enjoyed the luxury of electricity and the comfort it can bring along with running water and cooked meals. When we entered the infirmary, I quickly noticed a smile come to Quin's face. "Hello my friend." He said to me. "Quin, my buddy!" I replied as I rubbed his head in a gesture of friendship.

"Sorry for messing up your hair buddy, your full of bullet holes and I don't want to give you a hug for fear of you springing a leak!" I said as I laughed. He smiled back at my attempt at humor. He looked comfortable with an I-V drip in his left arm and surrounded by medical equipment the likes I have not seen in years. "They are taking good care of me Bo. I haven't had it this good in a long time." I sat in a chair beside his bed and as I looked at him, I thought back to the good times we had. "I'm so glad your recovering brother. I wish we could go out to happy hour tonight." Quin smiled and shook his head. "I'm ready for a good happy hour." He said. "I think you're going to be fine Quin and we will take a rain check on that happy hour. Hey Brother, I have to run and be on watch, but it is good to see you and I'll come back as soon as I can. We're heading to the Key's man! Remember we always used say we'd get there someday!" I said. Quin smiled and gave me a thumbs up as I quickly exited to my watch.

I was a soldier on watch on the battle cruiser Dreadnaught and I felt every bit of it. I was armed with a sidearm, a rifle, grenades, and long-range binoculars. It felt good but a bit strange. The ship was moving fast, and I felt rested and ready for whatever was to come.

As I peered out over the ocean from my post, I heard another sailor call out. "Boat activity at 3 O'clock!" The ship's Captain suddenly appeared and scanned the area with his binoculars. "Looks like someone fishing but keep an eye on it." This kind of activity kept on for several hours as the Dreadnaught kept plowing through the water. We continued a southernly course alongside the east coast of Florida. I could now make out the slight outline of a skyline of buildings in the far distance. I can only imagine the once bustling cities of Palm Beach, Ft Lauderdale, Miami, now only shadows of their former metropolises on this cloudless day.

As I was scanning the horizon, I suddenly heard a voice. "Beautiful out there isn't it?" I turned and saw the captain standing beside me. "Yes sir, it is." I replied.

"My first memory of the ocean was with my family at the beach. We lived in Atlantic Beach Florida. Probably just over that way." He said as he pointed toward the west. "My father was in the Navy and stationed in Mayport. I used to love going to the beach and playing in the waves." He stated. "Sounds nice sir." I replied. "Probably where I got my love for the ocean. Private Brown, I understand you're new to the military but not new to fighting. I appreciate your service."

"I'm glad to be here sir. I hope we can make a difference and get some semblance of our country back."

"It's a shame what has happened. I lost some good friends both from the fight and to the fight." The captain said. "Sir?" I asked to clarify. "I've had friends die fighting on both sides. Civil wars are never pretty. It tears apart the nation, it tears apart armies, and it tears apart families and friends." He said. I continued to gaze on my watch as the captain spoke to me.

"When I was a child, I dreamed of being a ship's Captain. I would look out over the beach waves and imagine what was across the horizon. I thought if I could just swim far enough and fast enough, I could swim to a new world someday." He said with a chuckle. "Of course, being a captain of a boat was my dream. I never imagined it would be like this." He said.

"It's a beautiful ocean sir." I said. "Yes, it is Private Brown, yes, it is."

My watch ended as the sun was beginning to set. I was lucky to continue with the day watch and it was nice that it remained uneventful. The captain explained that we should arrive at the Fort Zachary Cruise Pier by daylight the next morning. I bid my fellow watchmen so long for the day and made my way back to the infirmary to check in on Quin before heading to the mess hall and a needed shower. I loved every minute of this mission.

As I walked into the infirmary, I glanced at Quin whom I noticed was asleep. Beside him checking his I-V was one of the loveliest visions I had seen in a long time. She instantly smiled at me. "Hi" she said. "Hi"

I sheepishly replied. I must admit that I have had no interest in any ladies, nor had I had an opportunity to have interest since my Olivia. I must admit, this felt great.

"I'm Emma, the nurse for the infirmary. Can I help you?"

"I'm sorry, what is your name again?" I asked, quite distracted by her beauty.

"I am Nurse Emma Ford."

Emma's healthy red hair covered her shoulders in a fashion I had not seen in a very long time. She was stunningly attractive and even the way she handled the I-V bag seemed exquisitely elegant. She wore scrubs which appeared sexy yet appropriate.

"Quin is my buddy. We are old friends' way back to our time in New York." I said. I knew she had no idea what I was talking about. "I'm sorry my name is Bo." I said as I attempted an awkward introduction.

"Bo, can you grab me that blanket on the chair over there and that full I-V. I have to change this out." I handed her the blanket. "...and the I-V bag please."

"Oh yes, of course." I said with a sheepish grin. I watched her elegant and soft hands change the I-V bag and could not take my eyes off her slender attractive body. As she finished, she turned her head toward me sending her beautiful long red hair flowing across her shoulders in what appeared to be a slow-motion clip out of an old movie. I was mesmerized by her.

"You are very attractive." I admitted. "I apologize for being sheepish and flustered as I stand here. Seriously! Is that hair flinging thing something you do to all guys? I know that sounds stupid, but I really would like to go get cleaned up and meet you in the mess hall for a quick bite. Or maybe not so quick. What are my odds?" I asked with a sheepish grin on my face.

"You do know we are on a war ship in the middle of the ocean during a war right, uh, Bo?" She replied. Then suddenly she touched my arm gently and said with a gentle smile, "I'm just kidding Bo, your friend Quin told me all about you. I'll see you in thirty in the mess." Then she quickly left the room. As she left, I felt like all the air left the room. "Wow, what was that?" I glanced back at Quin who was now awake and looking at me with a smile. "It's about time my old friend. Go to her!" he said.

Thirty minutes later to the exact minute, I arrived at the mess hall and found her already sitting with a cup of coffee and a piece of toast on a small paper plate. She was chatting with another young soldier as she looked up and smiled at me. We greeted each other and I formally introduced myself once again and met the young man sitting at the table. She has been working as a nurse on the Dreadnaught since the beginning of the war. She explained to me that the ship was initially in the hands of the Freedom Party Regime until allies of the U.S Regime took it back and held it until we arrived. I gave her a brief history of myself while she shared half of her toast with me, and I sipped on a cup of water as we exchanged smiles and small compliments. Emma was a kind and sweet person. As I listened to her construct stories of her past and present, I realized that something was different. Her constant smile and her direct eye contact drew me to her like a warm magnetism. I felt a sense of easiness, calm, and reassurance like I have not felt in a very long time. Olivia continued to be on my mind as we spoke, but it was as if I felt a calm forgiveness from her or a strange push from a spirit to move on. I felt Olivia's presence, but I didn't share it with Emma.

Suddenly out of nowhere...my ease was shattered. The ship alarm went off and jolted everyone from a relaxed state to an extremely tense battle readiness. "Battle Stations! Battle Stations! Battle Stations!" came loudly over the intercom system. Emma looked at me as she touched my hand. No more words were exchanged as I backed away from her, turned and ran to my post.

Tobey and I met at our post almost simultaneously as we focused on an oncoming large vessel heading our way. The sun had just set but there was still a glow in the sky. Rapid gunfire began to erupt from the bow of the vessel as it headed directly toward us. "Let's sink that bastard!" Tobey yelled. "Same drill Bo!" I lifted the 55-pound projectile and handed it off to my team mate as previously and watched the men orchestrate loading it into the gun. "Fire!" I heard Tobey yell. The gun blasted the projectile toward the vessel but missed with a very large explosion only feet from vessels hull. Bullets were now ricocheting off the Dreadnaught as we continued this dance to destroy the oncoming enemy. I looked up and now saw several smaller vessels coming at us from different directions barely visible in the evening hue. Several of our crew members with automatic rifles began converging on the deck to fire upon them. The Dreadnaught began to turn as I lost my footing momentarily. I could feel our ship was in evasive maneuvers as we were going full speed and turning in rapid fashion in different directions. "Fire!" Tobey yelled. The gun blast was deafening and with each blast came a powerful concussion that seemed to suck in all the air around us. "They are too close to use the deck gun boys! Arm yourselves with rifles and fire at them!" Tobey yelled as bullets grazed the air around us. The sound of the automatic weapons was haunting. Rapid TAT, TAT, TAT, TAT, TAT, TAT seemed to come from everywhere and the sound of metal ricocheting off metal as the bullets hit around us. I was handed an M249 machine gun and began firing at the vessels. The disorganization of our defense seemed paralyzing.

"Tobey! We must make a coordinated effort to take these guys out! They're about to overwhelm us!" I yelled.

There were five enemy vessels coming at us from different angles out of the west from the mainland. Our cannon fire disabled one of the boats, but the large vessel and three others were starting to parallel the Dreadnaught and laying a lot of firepower.

I was becoming frustrated at our effort. "Tobey! Take three men and go forward!" I yelled. "I will remain here with the others and send a few men to the stern!"

Tobey and his three comrades took off toward the bow of the Dreadnaught. As I began to motion a few of the men I suddenly saw Sarge appear from around the corner. "Sarge, take cover!" I yelled as the bullets kept piercing the air. Sarge took cover as he struggled with a very large M60 machine gun he was carrying with both hands. He suddenly lifted the gun to the railing of the ship and began blasting away at the vessels beside us. I peered through a gap in the railing to watch the onslaught. A spray of bullets hit the water and then the boats as they appeared to take the impact of multiple rounds of bullets. It gave Tobey and I enough time to get our bearings and set our sights on the enemy combatants. I fired off in rapid succession and saw several men fall. Tobey and his men did the same. Sarge stood up and kept firing that machine gun like the battle worn hero that he was. I glanced back toward the stern to see if my comrades had gotten into a position to return fire. As I turned back around, I was astonished at the bravery of Sarge standing there rattling off that machine gun like a man possessed. Suddenly Sarge's gun fell silent as I watched in horror, several rounds hitting Sarge in the arm and chest area. His blood-spattered body fell against me. I gently pushed him aside as the bullets kept flying. I picked up the smoking M60 and carried on as Sarge was lying below me. I kept firing that large gun until I saw pieces of the boats breaking apart from the onslaught we were delivering. They began to back off as I continued to fire. The enemy was now retreating with several of their comrades floating in the dark waters of the warm Atlantic. I fell against the siding of the ship and tried to catch my breath. I felt the Dreadnaught turn to its original Southern course and cut the water like a knife as we continued to Key West. I turned my head towards Sarge and watched as he coughed blood. His eyes gazed at me as he managed a slight smile through his suffering. "We got those bastards." He said.

Chapter Eight

<u>Hero's & Hope</u>

I never really contemplated the definition of the word hero. Everyone's a hero in battle. If you are self-preserving yourself or another in the fog of war you don't have the opportunity to really think about it. A hero may be someone that is admired for courage or noble qualities but the person that is admired may not think of themself as a hero. Why? Because when you are in an act of self-preservation you don't have a chance to be anything but. Noble qualities notwithstanding, it is what it is.

Walking into an air-conditioned room from the hot humid air of Key West was amazing. Even in the fall months, South Florida is hot and humid. I relished the cool air despite the slight hint of a moldy scent in the old building. Mateo Garcia stood at the head of the old classroom. Captain Surles, Stan McKinley, Tobey Longstreet, and I gathered for the briefing.

"First and foremost, I want to welcome you all to Key West." Mateo Garcia said. "Captain, it looks as if your ship took on some fire on your journey from Charleston."

"The men did a fine job in defending her Mr. Garcia." The captain said. "We are very glad to be here, and I am proud of my crew.

Mateo Garcia was of proud Cuban ancestry and became the Mayor of Naples Florida six years ago prior to the civil war. He stood 5' 4" with a round build and loved to wear his tropical shirts that seemed to fit his laid back but arrogant personality. He would usually be found with a cigar in his mouth if he could find one.

"We have electricity being produced by our local plant, hot and cold running water, and plenty of supplies. I want you all to take advantage of our hospitalities and get some rest. However, before you rest, we have some things to discuss. I received notice from Commander Bell that you all would be arriving. I wasn't so sure. It is good to see you all here two days early. I would like to take this moment to allow Captain Surles to relay some Commendations from Commander Bell."

The Captain of the Dreadnaught stepped up and spoke.

"As I look out the window here in this old classroom, I see the Dreadnaught in port looking beaten but not down. We made it men! If it were not for your heroic actions, we may not be here. I would now like to recognize a few of you."

I stood thinking of Sarge. He was alive but obviously couldn't be here for this informal yet slightly ostentatious ceremony.

"Mr. Beauregard brown you played a vital role in carrying out your defensive position on the Dreadnaught and saving Sargent Harrisons life and fending off enemy combatants. For the vital and heroic role you played you will be promoted to the rank of Corporal and be awarded a Medal of Commendation. Congratulations Corporal Brown."

I stood and walked to Captain Surles and shook his hand. I felt numb with pride. "Thank you, sir. This was unexpected as I was just doing my duty." I said.

The captain smiled at me as I turned and rejoined my comrades.

"Sargent Harrison is recovering however he too will also be awarded a Commendation and be promoted to the rake of Lieutenant. He received some very harsh wounds, but we expect him to recover." The captain said.

Tobey and Stan also received Commendations for coming to the aid of the wounded and laying down extraordinary firepower despite the threat of personal sacrifice. Mr. Garcia shook our hands and patted us on the back as he pulled out a cigar. "I wish I had one for each of you, but I don't! He said. "Hard to come by you know." It was all smiles as I beamed in my newfound heroism. The ceremony was small and brief, but it felt good to be recognized for almost dying I suppose.

Mateo Garcia had to reach up high to put his arm around the 6'2" Tobey Longstreet. The Texas cowboy looked down at Mateo as the two lead the way out of the building and into an expansive yard with palm trees, flowering bougainvillea and the scent of honey suckle. Mateo exhaled cigar smoke that unfortunately overwhelmed and clouded the sweet scent of the honey suckle. "Follow me gentlemen to one of the most famous bars in Key West! Been open through the entire war!" Mateo said excitedly. We smiled and began following Mateo's blue haze of cigar smoke down the street to what felt like a refreshing adventure. Tobey gave a celebratory fist pump in cowboy fashion and Stan kicked up his heels showing his Irish gig talent. I turned and saw Captain Surles heading back toward the Dreadnaught, his head was held high, and his walk had a confident stride. I walked quickly to catch up with the gang. I smiled as I observed my new heroic comrades enjoying the walk along a busy Key West Street eagerly awaiting a long overdue drink in a local bar.

Since the war began and in the course of battles being won and lost, the Florida Keys and Key west have become a haven and safety net for soldiers, democracy seekers, artists, and many in the LGBTQ community seeking refuge from religious persecution and fascism. From central Florida on down the vibe of a democracy and freedom existed in a way I have not seen in years. With support of other countries helping with food, additional fresh water, fuel for the power plant and any other supplemental items needed to support the US reforming to a democratic state it was the hub of activity. I was extremely impressed and very glad to be here. I soon found out that in addition to myself and unit I was serving with, there were some very important folks here creating the foundations for our reformed country.

Mateo turned around as he was walking and grabbed the cigar out of his mouth. "Glad to have you boys here! I love this town!" He said. The breeze off the ocean felt great on the island. There were people sitting on the curb as we walked down the street. There were very few vehicles as gas was still hard to come by even here. Most everything was shipped in as many bridges had been destroyed in the battles. The only way to many of the Key's was by boat. That is the case for Key West, but it keeps it safe from the enemy and well-fortified. The people here are the lucky ones. They smile as they pass and even reach out to shake our hand knowing we are their line of defense. There are people from all walks of life. Older folks, young families, and it seemed many more ladies than men. I suppose the men either died or are off fighting in the north. We continued walking down the street being recognized from the hearsay of a small island town as well as the handguns we had strapped to our sides. We were not in uniforms for two reasons. One, uniforms make you stand out as a combatant and two, there were just no more uniforms to go around in a country where supplies were scarce.

We navigated our way down Greene Street following the continued haze of Mateo's cigar smoke. Passing once bustling tourist shops now used mostly for housing and the occasional resident attempting to sell their wares. We came upon a large sign above the entrance that read Captain Tony's Saloon topped by a large fish that was now riddled with bullet holes. It was 3:00 O'clock in the afternoon and several patrons were making their way into the large old double doors that served as the entrance. "Welcome to Captain Tony's Saloon!" Mateo busted out. "This is where the once great Earnest Hemingway got sloshed on many occasions! Let me buy you gentleman a few well deserved drinks!" Mateo offered.

The bar was a dark hole in the wall with what looked to be an old tree growing up through the middle of the room. It has the stench of old liquor and stale beer. A few men with sidearms strapped to their hip sat on bar stools and sipped their alcohol. One guy was shirtless and barefoot, but that was not unusual for this island town. We each took a bar stool and Mateo ordered a round of drinks made with the local rum and a splash of coconut milk. The bartender was eager to slap down the drinks in front of each of us. "Make sure you leave me the plastic cups boys, I reuse them." He stated.

"I haven't had a drink since I left Texas! Yeehaw!" Tobey yelled out with a wave of his cowboy hat. "Here's to the best warhorse in the land! To Tabasco!" Tobey yelled. "I miss that damn horse." "To a jolly good horse!" Stan said in his Irish accent. A man across the bar took notice and raised his cup. "Thank you, men, for the job, service, and sacrifice that you are living to get our country back." The man said.

Mateo stared at the man for a moment. "Colonel Hatcher is that you sir?"

"In the flesh and blood gentlemen." Mateo stood up and began introductions. "Gentlemen, this is Colonel Ivan Hatcher. He is responsible for over taking the Dreadnaught from the enemy and giving you a ship to get here on." I looked over to the other side of the bar as did Tobey and Stan. Tobey raised his cup of coconut rum to the Colonel and shouted, "Here's to killing insurrectionists!" We all chuckled, raised our cups, and drank down the nectar. "I'm ready for another!" I yelled out.

The camaraderie lasted for several hours as we drank down the rum drinks with gusto. I got to know my comrades and even had a long chat with Colonel Hatcher. It was a great experience and fun I hadn't seen in several years.

It isn't as if I felt the need for alone time after our happy hour at Captain Tony's, but I found myself taking a long walk to the old marina as the sun was setting. My Medal of Commendation was tucked securely in my front pocket. When I reached the marina, I was surprised to find more sailboats than I could count. It was as if everyone decided the way to escape the madness was to go to sea. Sailboats were double and triple rafted together at the docks to make as much room as possible. Many others appeared in the harbor moored to mooring buoys with their masthead lights glowing in the distance. It gave the look of stars on the water. I suppose the Keys and South Florida gave refuge from the profuse fighting and anguish the rest of the country was experiencing.

"Hey you there!" I heard a voice call out.

As I turned to see where the voice was coming from, I saw a familiar face. Walking toward me I saw Emma. She was smiling and walking with both hands in the pockets of her short cutoff blue jeans. Her long legs had a nice stride that I admired. Her head had a slight tilt as she suddenly whipped her head to throw her hair back over her right shoulder. She looked damn good and if I didn't know better, she appeared to be smiling and walking as if to flirt with me.

"Emma, the nurse!" I said as I began to smile back.

"Bo, the hero!" She replied. "How about we put formalities aside and just make it Emma and Bo."

I agreed and for the moment I suddenly had that feeling back again. It was a great feeling. All thoughts of war, all thoughts of anguish and sorrow seemed to lift away. Maybe it was still the rum but whatever, I liked the feeling. We found ourselves walking a bit and ended up sitting on a sea wall not far from the marina. The profusion of masthead lights appeared to be dancing on the water to a guitar we heard playing in the distance. A sound I have not heard for a while.

"It's hard to believe this world is such a disturbed place." She said. I looked at her as I was slowly feeling the buzz of the rum fading.

"Do you really think it is? I'm not so sure Emma." I replied. I'm not sure where the sudden positive and confident feeling I had was coming from, but I suppose it was her. She looked back at me with a slight smile.

"We've lost everything in this damn war. People we loved, a country. What gives you the feeling this is not a disturbed and dreadful place?" She asked me.

I chuckled and thought of what to say next as I looked out over the lights in the harbor, the distant guitar music, and then back at her beautiful face.

"I suppose your right in many ways Emma, but we are still alive, and we have lost many things, no actually most of everything, but..." I suddenly paused and looked into her eyes.

At that moment I did something regrettably stupid. As we sat on that seawall with our legs kicking out over the water like a couple of kids, I leaned into her beautiful face and kissed her. Emma slightly kissed back but I could tell there was hesitation. I slowly back away.

"Your timing is a little off, but I appreciate the kiss." She said.

"I'm so sorry Emma."

"Don't be sorry Bo. I like you. I especially like the fact that you can express hope."

I smiled and shook my head to air my regret.

"I do believe in hope Emma, and I believe this war is coming to an end. I've seen it and I feel it."

"I've seen a lot of wounded and dying soldiers Bo and I know you have as well. I'm just not there yet. Do you know what tyranny of the majority is?" She asked. I had no idea what she was talking about. "It's when the will of a majority population exclusively prevails in a governmental system. The result is tyranny over minority groups. It's basically what happened to our society however the minority groups happened to be us."

I had to absorb what she just said. I thought a lot about that, the problem was, is that most people were tired of over analyzing the causes of the war and I for one was ready to have it over. In addition, I just wasn't sure I agreed.

"Emma, explain something to me. If a majority prevails in government, why would there be tyranny?" I asked. She smiled at me again enjoying the engagement.

"Because the majority may not necessarily be most of the people but the majority that came into power. In other words, those that have the ability to shape policy excluding others from those benefits which they have chosen. Bo, the Freedom Manifesto was the beginning. Then the Freedom Party of America gained power through convincing the masses that the country was in a moral and religious decay. Once these people were in power, they deceived everyone for their own gain. And what was their gain? Not kindness, love or giving, but hate and moral turpitude. Bo, I know you know this and I'm sorry, I'm so sorry I'm carrying on."

She was right about it all. I smiled at her and touched her hand. "You speak with a passion Emma. It's admirable." I said.

"No, what's admirable is you. Bo the hero."

At that moment she leaned in and gave me a kiss. Not a long kiss but a very nice surprise soft kiss. We ended our short get together as I walked her back to the ship. The walk was quiet and peaceful. I had a feeling she wanted it that way. Every now and then I caught her glancing my way with a smile. Once back aboard the Dreadnought I found myself not wanting to leave her side. It was so enjoyable being with her. She looked at me and took my hand. "Thank you, Bo the hero." She gave me another gentle kiss and then turned and went her way.

Your very welcome, Emma the nurse." I replied.

The seasons never really change in the Florida Keys. When winter arrives in Key West, the humidity is less, and the evenings are pleasantly cool but as far as a true turn of the seasons like I felt in the northeast it was nonexistent. I was not complaining. This area was once a playground for the northern retirees to come and enjoy a gleeful time of year away from the cold and snow of the north, today it is a haven away from the struggles of survival and the anguish of battle. Amazing efforts have been made to continue fresh water and electricity to this part of the country and from what I understand it continues to get better with power, water and hope being restored to several parts of the country to the north. The Dreadnaught left to accomplish further missions along the east coast along with Emma. I missed her. Emma and I had made a connection I had not felt since my darling Olivia. I suppose we would call it love but Emma and I knew the reality we were in, and she was right about so many things. She called me a dreamer, a romantic, someone trying to live in a different time and often referred to an old song by Bob Segar called "Against the Wind." Well, perhaps I am running against the wind but if I am, so are many others as well and that gives me hope. It only made me miss Emma even more.

Four months had quickly passed by since Emma and the Dreadnaught had left. I was quartered in a small two-bedroom housing unit at the Naval Air Station along with Tobey and my old friend Quin Rodriguez who was now healed from the wounds he sustained on our way to Charleston. The base was small and old but in relatively good condition. The tropical location was amazing, and I considered myself extremely lucky. We were now under the charge of Colonel Hatcher who at the time unbeknownst to us was working on a continuity plan to restore the United States along with major leaders and players. Key West had become a strategic and political jumping off point. It was now populated mostly with soldiers, some freedom fighters from other countries, many refugees, families, artists, and shop keepers. We just happened to be at the right place at the right time. Sarge was now out of action. We heard he recovered in a hospital in Ft. Myers and was now living on a vegetable farm near Homestead. I was able to visit him briefly while on a security mission and he was still in a wheelchair and working with a physical therapist to hopefully walk again. His future was grim. I am sure he misses the action and his men from the Virginia National Guard. But in my world, history was beginning to unfold in a positive manner and being the dreamer I was, I felt hope was on the horizon.

Chapter Nine

The Virginia National Guard had adopted me, and I had adopted them. If this had not occurred, I suppose I would still be trying to carve out an existence on my parent's old homestead in West Virginia, but things were changing. The Virginia National Guard that had found me over a year ago had merged into several other units. The leader of this hodgepodge army was Colonel Hatcher. Hatcher was taking his orders from none other than the famous General Sean Bishop. There were other leaders and other players but much of the planning was secret and above my pay grade.

"Get up Bo! There's a briefing by General Bishop in thirty minutes at the Monkey House!" I heard Quin yell as I was enjoying the last few minutes of sleep. The Monkey House is the name the men gave to the meeting quarters on base because we all sometimes thought of ourselves as trained monkeys.

"There's an extra cup of Cuban coffee on the table to get you going." He said. The Cubans had supplied our army with enough coffee to feed a nation. It was an amazingly strong brew that stood your hair on end and would give me the shakes as if I was on a bender.

I got myself up and downed the strong coffee. "Nice!" I felt my heart skip a few beats, but I was awake.

"What's up with a briefing by Bishop?" I asked.

Quin grabbed a few last items and threw them in his backpack. "I don't know but let's go."

"Where's Cowboy Tobey?" I asked. "He's already gone and on his way. Let's go!"

These briefings usually involved the selection of teams for either a short reconnaissance mission or providing security and protection to infrastructure crews throughout Florida. This is what I have been doing over the past three months. This one was obviously different as the brass were showing up.

When we arrived at the Monkey House a gathering of soldiers were taking seats with only a few seats left in the back. Quin and I quickly sat down as we watched Hatcher and Bishop walk to the front of the room. The room grew quiet as Colonel Hatcher began to speak.

"Ladies and Gentlemen, I thank you all for being here this morning as we have some important news to share with you. I'm sure some of you have heard that we have been working on an alliance with other states to gain ground as well as a continuity plan to reestablish a democratic government. You all here in key West are at the forefront of this effort. I would now like to turn it over to General Bishop who will brief you all on these efforts."

Hatcher and Bishop were very similar to each other. Both wore a uniform sharply and both had that career military look about them, poker faced, stern, upright, and no nonsense. Hatcher had an Army background while Bishop was a Marine. That didn't seem to matter anymore. General Bishop walked to the front of the room. He was a well-built black man approximately fifty-two years old. No one really knew the full story of his escape from the Hughes regime, but the man had a history, an amazing history and story. I began to listen intently.

"Ladies and Gentlemen, we have made some extraordinary strides in defeating the insurgence. We now almost have exclusive control of Florida and much of Georgia. The insurgency is on the run and continues to surrender as we speak. We have military cohesiveness within the four major branches and are gaining stability. With that said, we have begun and will continue to rebuild infrastructure so this nation can again be a nation of freedom and free ourselves from tyranny. Within the next fifteen days many of you will support a mission to overtake the District of Columbia and surrounding area. This includes most of Virginia, Delaware, and Maryland. We have taken the fight to the insurgency, and they are losing. Now is the time to strike and take our country back. Ladies and gentlemen, our founding fathers would be ashamed as to what has happened in this country but would be proud of your fight. The hard work and genius that they put into our founding constitution was the framework for a great nation. I believe it can and will be again. You men and women have fought hard. We have made many sacrifices and there will be many more to make. The children of tomorrow are counting on us. With that said I would like to answer any questions."

A young lady toward the front raised her hand and General Bishop pointed to her.

"Yes, and thank you Sir, how much of the state now has power and is fuel available for transport?"

"The State of Florida has power through Tampa and Orlando areas, and I believe we are gaining more every day. Fuel is now available on a limited basis through these areas for vehicle transport. Pipelines continue to be constructed and repaired coming from Texas and the west. Most of these regions are now insurgent free. Our allies continue to supply us with the valuable fuel we need. Ladies and Gentlemen, we are winning!"

Quin raised his hand as General Bishop looked his way and pointed to him.

"Sir, what is the objective of replacing the Hughes Regime? Is there a plan for a new presidency?"

"Yes, there is. As I stated previously, we are winning this war and the Hughes Regime is failing. Once we retake the former Capitol and liberate the surrounding areas a vote will be cast for a new president. Ladies and Gentlemen, we will build a new nation!"

One last question was asked by a front row participant, "Sir, where is Hughes?"

"Gerald Hughes is thought to be in the Washington D.C. area. We know he resided in the White House after he became President, but we are not exactly sure of his location on this date. We will get him."

When the briefing was over, I was summoned by my new direct commander Lieutenant John Beck. I had known Lieutenant Beck for some time now since our attack on Charleston. He and his men helped Sarg and our group get to the Dreadnaught. Beck was a tall skinny man originally from Norfolk Virginia. He was the offspring to a Navy family and followed in their footsteps. He joined the Virginia National Guard once the war started and took the side of the Union. He claimed to be a religious man and he didn't like the way the regime had used faith and religion as bait to claim the more ignorant to the side of the insurgency. He spoke softly but had a very tough demeanor. He came across as a good leader. I was told he played basketball at the Virginia Military Institute and was pretty good for a white man. I shrugged off the white man comment and just thought I would love to challenge him sometime.

Beck enjoyed meeting with us in a small park just outside the base. The tropical air, swaying palms, and green grass allowed us to feel more at ease. I'm not sure if this was a curse or a benefit. Once we arrived at the park I noticed Cowboy Tobey, that's what I started calling Longstreet, Cowboy Tobey Longstreet. Cowboy Tobey was strolling up with his ten-gallon Texas hat on his head and a strip of honeysuckle vine in his mouth. His handgun strapped tightly to his leg. You can take the man out of Texas, but you can't take the Texas out of the man. I smiled at him.

"Well hello Boys! Don't ya'll have a warm and fuzzy feeling in your gut after hearing Bishop's pep talk? I'm gunna sit right here and grab a patch of grass. Beautiful day! I think we are gunna go hunt us some insurrectionists boys!"

I just shook my head as I smiled. I liked Tobey. He was a good soldier but a pain in the ass to live with. He shot off his handgun in our housing unit one night after a woman at Captain Tony's spurned him. It took a while to calm him down. He also had a fetish for cross bows, his weapon of choice when ammo was low. I told him the story of how I witnessed marauders shooting an arrow through the head of my new friend Thomas. It didn't faze Cowboy as he shrugged it off as another death in a bitter war. Also present were my roommates Quin, and Stan McKinley.

It was another beautiful day on the island. Lieutenant Beck arrived, and we stood up to greet him.

"Good afternoon gentlemen, as you have heard from the General, we have a new mission."

Beck began to speak and described our part of the mission as reconnaissance but before he could finish Stan interrupted. "This is it, Lieutenant? Where is everybody else?"

"You are it Gentlemen. This will be a reconnaissance mission that requires only a small team. You all have been selected." Beck continued.

"We will be infiltrating enemy territory to find and report back enemy positions. We are also to report back the status of living conditions, economic conditions, fuel supplies, weapon supplies and anything else of vital importance. Gentlemen, I don't have to tell you that this will be a very important but dangerous mission. We will ship out in forty-eight hours on the shrimping vessel Valiant. Each of you will be led ashore at different intervals in different locations to ascertain the conditions in as many areas as possible. The plan is to rendezvous at a prearranged point and time. So, that's the plan in a nutshell gentleman. I will give more specifics as the need arises or if it changes. What you do with your time between now and then is up to you but when you arrive at the Valiant be timely, be rested, and be ready."

The lieutenant then turned and walk off.

"Damn boys, I guess we won't be hunting insurrectionists after all! We'll be walking among them!" Cowboy said.

"Bloody hell!" said Stan.

I wasn't sure what to think. I was proud to be among these men but at the same time we were all tired of the fight. I took a deep breath and suddenly realized the importance of the mission. I was truly doing something and a part of something that was much larger than I could imagine.

"Anybody want to go fishing?" Stan asked.

"We have 48 hours guys. I suggest we use them wisely." I said.

Corporal Bo, I suggest we go to Captain Tony's and get our drunk on!" Cowboy said.

I smiled as I just wasn't used to the sound of Corporal at this point. "That sounds like a plan Cowboy!" Stan replied. "Well of course it would to you Irish! And quit calling me Cowboy, my name is Tobey!"

It was still early in the day, and I wasn't ready to get my drunk on yet, so I decided to walk around the small island and contemplate the next mission. "I'll catch up with guys. Don't take all the pretty women!" I said.

I found myself walking along Whitehead Street and ended up at the southernmost point in the continental United States. A large cement marker in the shape of a buoy marked the spot. I sat on the seawall and watched the water glistening in the beautiful fall sun. I thought about Olivia and called out to her.

"Olivia if you can hear me know that I think of you every day. I miss you and life has been a struggle without you. God, I loved you." A lone seagull flew low to the water and suddenly began to glide in the air as if speaking to me. I wondered.

I slowly walked along through this pleasant tropical town as I watched a couple of roosters chase each other across the street. I chuckled to myself. There are a lot of Roosters and chickens in Key West. The locals consider them sacred and frown upon killing and eating them although it has become necessary at times. I turned the street corner and suddenly and without warning I saw some familiar faces.

"Danny! Brenda!"

"Oh my gosh!" Brenda said.

I haven't seen Danny or Brenda since the Dreadnaught left and I just assumed they were still aboard.

"Wow! It's so good to see you guys! I thought you left the island on the Dreadnaught!" We proceeded to give each other long hugs.

"No! no! We've been housed in a small unit about mid island. Danny has been working at the marina and on the fuel dock and I help run a small kitchen on Duval Street." Brenda said as her hands started shaking.

"Oh, don't mind the shaking it's my nerves." She said with a smile.

"You are a sight for sore eyes buddy! What is going on with you? I understand we are winning the fight?" Danny asked.

"Danny I'm doing everything possible to help us win this war!" I said with a grin.

It was so good to see this couple. I often think about them and how if it wasn't for Danny and Brenda I wouldn't be where I am today.

"Listen, I am heading back to my quarters to get cleaned up and changed. I'm going to meet Toby, Quin, and Stan at Captain Tony's. You guys must join us!"

"We would love to! I want to catch up." Danny said.

I made my way back to my quarters, opened the fridge, took out a bottle of Cristal, and took a sip. It's been an interesting day. I suppose I should make my way to Captain Tony's but first I thought I would write a quick letter to Emma. Mail was sporadic at best, but I knew the army had now set up its own internal mail system. We had already corresponded a few times and it was evident that a few of our letters had gone astray. I thought I'd give it a try anyway and without divulging our mission this was the letter:

Dear Emma the Nurse,

I'm thinking of your smile as I am writing this. Your gentle nature, your spirit, and the calming effect you have on me are missed dearly. Cowboy and Stan send their love. Quin is back to his old self, and you would not recognize him as the guy you nursed backed to health on the

Dreadnaught. I hope you and that old ship are doing well. I know with you as the ships nurse the men are in good hands. I just came back from a walk down to the sea wall on the southernmost point and thought about the evening we had at the marina. Maybe I think too much. You called me a dreamer once, as did my mother. Maybe there is something to be said about dreamers. It is a tough world out there, but my gut is telling me things will get better. Me and the guys have a tough mission coming up and I just wanted to let you know that I am thinking of you, and I will continue thinking of you. I am looking forward to the day when we can sit on that sea wall again. Don't worry about me. In fact, let's make a deal. You don't worry about me, and I won't worry about you. If only that could be true. I worry about you constantly. I hope you feel the same. I better run. Oh! I ran into Brenda and Danny on the street today amongst the chickens! Who would have guessed? I thought they were still helping on the Dreadnaught! I better run as we are all meeting up at Captain Tony's. I truly wish you were here. I hope to hear from you soon, Yours Bo.

Chapter Ten

<u>The Mission</u>

Captain Jim and his crew on the shrimp boat Valiant were proud to assist the cause. The Valiant along with a fleet of five other boats fished in the waters off the east coast for years. These men loved the sea and were glad to be here. Seafood became a staple when most of the red meat industry and factories collapsed because of the war. The shrimp boats were a common sight off the coast and would rarely draw a fight or suspicion from either side. It was excellent cover for our mission.

We had decided to go ashore in pairs rather than alone. Beck changed his mind after he thought about it. It's always good to have support in a combat situation even if you're only surveilling. Cowboy and I would be dropped off first near Alexandria and Irish and Quin would be dropped to the north near Annapolis.

Cowboy looked his part. The hat, boots, old dirty blue jeans, and flannel shirt that had the pocket ripped off.

"I'm ready to go ashore Lieutenant but should I wear my gun or conceal it in my waist band?"

"Your waistband looks a little too tight there Cowboy!" Stan said.

"Irish, you should you talk!" Cowboy replied.

"You all will wear your handguns and knives. The enemy will be armed. There is no distinction between soldier and civilian so watch your back. Everyone fights but be especially wary of uniforms." Lt. Beck replied.

It took some time for me to warm up to Stan McKinley also now known as "Irish". He's a nice guy but a little on the arrogant side. He immigrated from Ireland soon after President Brimley was assassinated indicating he was sick of Christian Nationalist taking over the world. I'm still not clear what his agenda was in America but I'm glad he's on our side. He's quite a bulldog considering he stands about 5'4". He's got the build of a weightlifter and I want him on my side in a fight and in fact he often has been. His sandy colored hair gives him the look of a California surfer. The ladies love him. His thick Irish accent gives him away in an instant but he's fun to be with in a bar. The one thing I can appreciate about Irish is that I always know where he stands, and he won't back down.

Two 12-foot fishing skiffs pulled aside the Valiant. I realized that if the union would happen it would happen on the backs of these guys. We were greeted by several men ready to take us to our destinations. The optimistic sound in their voices gave us reason to be confident. I shook the hands of my comrades as we boarded and headed off into two separate directions.

My first impression of being ashore in enemy territory was not all that different from what I had experienced as I traveled through New York to West Virginia. There was a dark and grim feeling about the area. Cowboy and I thought it would be better to walk separately so we kept about fifty feet distance between ourselves. The streets were mostly empty other than a few people that seemed to be homeless perhaps looking for food or shelter. We knew gangs were ever present, so we watched our backs. Our first contact was to be with a man named Spike. It sounded to me like a dog's name but who am I to judge. We made our way to West Annapolis and through a neighborhood area that still held some charm. The Naval area was crawling with regime soldiers, but the accolades of the Academy had longed vanished since the military institutions collapsed during the coup. Bean Rush café sat in what was once a classic Virginian home. We walked in together and Cowboy surprised me by yelling a loud "Good morning, folks!" across the eatery.

"Have a seat gentleman, we don't have electricity today, but I have hot coffee off the fire, and I can make some fresh homemade toast with jam. All I ask in return is splitting some firewood in the back." The elderly lady replied.

"Ma'am that would be just fine." I replied. The house only occupied by one other frail looking lady staring at us while she sipped her coffee.

We finished up our coffee, not Cuban by the way, and the delicious homemade toast and made our way to the back of the house to pay our dues.

"Gentlemen, over here."

A tall thin elderly man gestured for us to follow him. I looked at Cowboy with suspicion.

"Spike?" Cowboy asked.

The man simply shook his head in an affirmative gesture, and we followed him into a small old garage area.

"Come on in here men. I surely appreciate all you do and your sacrifices." Spike said.

He pulled out a small flask and gestured toward us. "You want a nip?"

Cowboy smiled, grabbed the flask, and took a swig. I wasn't so inclined with a mission on my mind and a long day ahead. Spike took the flask from Cowboy and took a big swig himself. "Homemade whiskey!"

With the whiskey greeting out of the way Spike showed us a map of the town and current placements of regime soldiers and the best way for us to make to D.C. Spike led us to a couple of old bicycles.

"I ain't rode too many bicycles. You don't happen to have a horse around here, do you?" Cowboy asked. "No sir, but you can have this." Spike handed him the flask of whiskey. Cowboy took the whiskey, I grabbed the bikes and then I gladly split a few logs of wood for the elderly couple, and we were on our way.

The dark, grim feeling started to fade. Hope and faith are something that I feel America was built upon. As we traveled through the Virginia countryside we were greeted by people with a friendly smile and even a wave. The people didn't know our purpose. In fact, I would say we looked a little out of sorts traveling down the rode on bicycles, but I suppose there was no normal anymore. What gave me confidence in the hope and faith of the people were the smiles and waves and the need for comfort. Perhaps it gave our mission purpose.

The city of Washington D.C. in the best of times was a place where political aspirations either thrive or die. The power struggles are real here. Rewards are given for loyalty and prices are paid for treachery. In a time of war and especially in a time of tyranny, trust is only another word. In fact, it means nothing.

Cowboy and I gave up our bicycles to a gang in exchange for passage into the city limits a few miles back. We kept our calm as we thought a fight may jeopardize our cover. We were now on foot and made our way to our next contact in a small townhouse only a few blocks from the White House. As we walked by the White House, I was dismayed by the burned-out ruins that once stood as America's House. The front lawn held the scars of bomb craters, and the once majestic front lawn fountain was now a pile of rubble. I noticed that Cowboy took off his hat as we walked by, and he took a swig from his whiskey flask. He passed it to me, and I took a swig.

"Let's sit down for a minute, shall we?" I asked. We found an old park bench and sat down.

"This mission is a conflict of highs and lows." I said. Cowboy wiped is brow and put is hat back on.

"You know Bo, when I was a boy, my Daddy would put me on a horse and just said ride em'! I say that because sometimes you never know what kind of horse your gunna get."

"Damn Cowboy sometimes you can say the simplest things that make sense out of the most complicated of situations."

"This ain't complicated Bo. This is just war. This is simply just riden' out a wild ass horse. It'll break, sure enough. We're gunna tame this bitch. And then all you do is get back up and ride. It'll take some time, but you'll see."

"Unfortunately, Cowboy a lot of people ran out of time."

"True, that's very true my friend." Cowboy said.

We continued our walk toward Georgetown where we would camp down for the night in a park near the Potomac River. The presence of armed men standing on the street corners started giving us an uneasy feeling, so we changed our route to access back streets. It was the beginning of late afternoon and a cold front pushing through gave way to cloudy skies and brisk wind. As we rounded a corner, we saw a familiar but unsettling sight. Three young punks were shoving and hassling two women.

"I'm gunna take these assholes out." Cowboy said.

"Slow down Cowboy. We don't need any undue attention."

"I'm tired of this shit man. We can't just let this happen."

As we got closer to the men, or I should say, to the boys, they looked our way.

"You don't want none of this!" One of the boys said. They couldn't have been more than fifteen years old. The ladies looked in their mid-thirties, dressed well and were very attractive, obvious targets. The boys were very disheveled looking.

Cowboy wasn't having any of this. He walked a quick pace toward the boys and drew his side arm.

"I've got a bead on you boy! Who wants to die first?"

The boys were armed with only small knives.

"I'm serious punks! You got three seconds." And with that the boys fled.

I wasn't pleased with Cowboy, yet I also knew something had to be done.

"You could've jeopardized our mission man!'

"But I didn't."

The ladies were obviously shaken as we approached.

"We are not going to hurt you. Are you ok?" I asked.

"Yes, thank you. I am so glad heroes still exist." The brunette said. I smiled and began to turn to go when Cowboy chimed in.

"Ma'am my name is Tobey, and this here is Bo."

I started to get anxious and annoyed with Cowboy's flirtatious banter.

"Thank you, Gentlemen, for helping us out of that situation. Those young boys don't have a chance. My name is Janet, and this is Nicole."

Ok, so Janet was the brunette and Nicole was the blonde. I had to get Cowboy out of here. I was surprised they were even talking to us given our disheveled looks and Cowboy's, well, Cowboy look.

The ladies began to get more comfortable and smiled at us.

"Tobey and Bo, we were just returning from a local market where I picked up some cheese and apple cider. Would you gentlemen like to join us for a snack? I'm sure my husband would like to thank you as well and I know he would like to meet you." Janet said.

Cowboy didn't hesitate and before I could speak, he accepted, and we began walking towards Janet's townhouse in Georgetown.

Washington has seen a lot of fighting. The White House had been burned down. The Capital was bombed out but still held some functioning offices. Surprisingly the Mall looked ok but for the unkept lawn and tents for the refugees. The exclusive areas such as Georgetown were bullet riddled with burned out cars along the once prestigious streets. It was interesting to see horses tied up behind several of the homes. Perhaps the homes of more prominent soldiers or officers.

As we approached the townhouse, I had an uneasy feeling. Cowboy seemed oblivious as he continued to chat with Janet and Nicole. Don't get me wrong, the two ladies were lovely, and I was looking forward to some good cheese and fresh West Virginia apple cider. I just felt like we were getting off task. Cowboy pulled me aside noticing my uneasiness.

"Look Bo, we have an opportunity here. I know we don't know who these people are, but they don't know who we are either. We are in the hornet's nest here and I think we have an opportunity to exploit it. Let's ride this horse buddy and see where it takes us."

I knew Cowboy was right. This is what we were here for. I just hoped I could stay on the horse as well as he could. I agreed to go along.

Janet opened her front door and as we walked in it was very impressive. A large entry way gave way to an open living space and large side rooms. The first thing I noticed was the large chandelier hanging above us as we walked in, and it was on, as in a bright light. This place had electricity. Once again, Cowboy didn't hesitate.

"Well, I'll be a dusty boot! You have electricity!"

Janet smiled and gave a chuckle. "Yes, we are very fortunate to have a generator. My husband can obtain such things as well as fuel."

We followed the ladies into the home, and they asked us to take a seat in a large formal sitting area. Very Colonial, I thought to myself, how ironic.

"Let me take these grocery items to the kitchen and get you men something to drink. It's the least we can do. My husband Paul will be home shortly."

Cowboy and I sat in large formal chairs and couldn't have looked more out of place. I think at one point Cowboy started to chuckle under his breath as he tried to get in a comfortable position.

Nicole seemed like a sweet lady. Not as talkative as Janet but very pleasant. It was obvious these people had connections and had access to material things through either money, bartering or power. My guess would be the latter.

Janet walked in with glasses of apple cider atop a serving tray. Something I haven't seen in some time. "Here we go. This is fresh apple cider gentlemen. My husband loves it." Janet said as she offered up the goodness.

We all heard the front door open, and a man quickly walked through the entry way not noticing he had visitors.

"Paul!" Janet yelled out to him.

When the sharply dressed man made his appearance in the room I almost choked on my cider.

"Paul these nice gentlemen rescued Nicole and I from some thugs today. I invited them for some cheese and cider. Some boys I hadn't seen before tried to rob us with a knife and Tobey scared them away. We owe them our gratitude."

The man looked at Tobey and then looked over to me. His stare was chilling. My heart was about to pound through my chest.

"Gentlemen this is my husband Mr. Paul Blair."

Paul Blair...the same Paul Blair I met at Austin's wedding years before. Cowboy and I stood to greet the man.

"Gentlemen, nice to meet you. I'd love to hear all about what happened." He said.

The man shook our hands.

"First I would like us to pray together." Blair said.

We then circled hand in hand and Blair led the prayer.

"Dear Heavenly Father, it appears we owe a debt of gratitude to these men that are gracing my presence oh dear Lord. Please bestow upon them all the blessings you have for saving my beautiful wife Janet along with her kind friend Nicole. I ask that you bring torture and death to those that trespassed upon them today and may their end be swift. Finally, oh dear Lord, I thank you for the wonderful gifts you continue to bring upon this household and for the delicious cheese and apple cider that we have placed in front of us. Amen.

As Blair brought his head up, he looked at Cowboy.

"Sir where are you from?" he asked.

Cowboy looked at Paul Blair and paused.

"I'm from Texas sir, God bless Texas!"

Paul Blair continued to stare at Cowboy to the point he grew uncomfortable. Then he spoke.

"I don't know how they do things in Texas sir but here in my blessed home a man removes his hat in the home, in the presence of ladies and especially during a prayer!"

Cowboy quickly took his hat off and apologized profusely.

"And where are you from sir?" Blair asked me.

"West by God Virginia sir." I said.

"I appreciate what you have done. I've told these ladies many times not to go out unescorted. Janet, I forbid you to leave the house until I say so. Nicole, I appreciate you keeping my wife company, but I think it is time for you to leave."

Janet spoke out, "Paul, I've asked Nicole to stay for dinner."

"Janet, as the man of the house I have spoken. Again, thank you gentlemen for what you have done and may God bless you. I am a very busy man and must take care of some business. Janet, please see them out."

With that said, Nicole, Cowboy, and I were escorted from the building. Nicole only lived a block away and we gladly made sure she got home safely. Cowboy and I walked along the Potomac River just contemplating what happened.

"I've met that man before." I said to Cowboy.

"What?"

"I've met that man several years back at a friend's wedding. He was a key figure with the Freedom Party and from I remember he was the campaign manager for Stanley Brimley."

"That man is an ass." Cowboy said.

"Well said Cowboy. I do believe we have just made an amazing contact though. I don't think he remembered me."

Cowboy and I found a tight space in some grass behind a cement barricade in what was once the Georgetown Waterfront Park. It is now refuge for us and several other homeless individuals escaping the cold and the storm that was to come. And a storm was coming.

Chapter Eleven

<u>Finish the Mission</u>

They say time heals all wounds. Time does not heal the minds of mad men. Cowboy and I have grown close over the last three weeks on mission. When you have one ally in a world of enemies you can't help but become dependent on your comrade. The atmosphere was changing. Our observations indicated that the regime had all but collapsed. People were revolting against the Hughes Administration and his ideology. The principles and values for which people fought have been proven false.

Janet and Nicole have befriended us. At one point they thought we may even be spies. We never exposed our identity however we 've gained each other's trust. Who could blame them. They lived in a world of tyranny and hate. The day that we rescued the ladies from the thugs was a lucky day. The happenstance that we came across Paul Blair was just, well, a pure miracle.

Nicole Ford gave us refuge in a small shed in the back of her large home. It afforded space for a small franklin stove that provided warmth from the winter cold. The idea to send a reconnaissance team into Washington D.C in the winter from the warm comfort of south Florida was not well thought-out but the importance of the mission called for it. Nicole's husband worked for the regime as a close advisor to Hughes and accepted our being on his property provided, we helped with some renovations as well as run errands. It fit well with our scheme. Cowboy was playing his role well and I believe at some point he may have had an affair with Janet. I kept thinking this was unlikely but even Cowboy had a penchant for love around his rough edges. The mission was full of surprises.

We had communication from Key West by way of a network of resistance collaborators. This was convenient yet very risky. With the tide turning against the regime, it was easier to gain support, but you always had to question who you could trust. Our most recent communication indicated they wanted us to return to Key West. Cowboy and I didn't like that idea. We had an inside path and knew we had to stay the course. The Hughes Regime was disoriented, confused and very sloppy. The resistance in the areas they still controlled was gaining more strength daily and we felt we were in a really good position to make a difference. I sent word to Key West that we were staying.

With the traditional Thanksgiving Holiday on the horizon the Blairs had asked that Cowboy and I take a couple of horses and try to commandeer a turkey. We found it quite comical yet hypocritical that they would continue to celebrate a traditional holiday to give thanks.

We made our way to a local poultry farm where we met a gentleman by the name of Cliff Smith who ran Capitol Hill Poultry. When we explained what we needed he was very reluctant and argumentative.

"This is no time to be celebrating a holiday to give thanks!" Mr. Smith said. "People are starving, and you want a damn turkey for Thanksgiving?"

Mr. Smith was adamant that he was not going to give up a turkey without a fight.

"Mr. Smith, let me explain our situation." I said.

We had a wonderful conversation with Mr. Smith and explained to him who we were and what our plan was. We did not like giving up our identities but felt this was important. Once again, we had another ally and not just one, Mr. Smith happened to be the leader of the local resistance force.

Cliff Smith was a tall slender gentleman with slightly graying hair and always was seen wearing overalls. He appeared to me as the stereotypical farmer as he walks with a slight limp and a hunched over back. Apparently, the result of the abuse he endured from years of farming. He raised chickens for meat as well as for eggs. Turkeys and a few swine were also part of his farm however not the predominant livestock. His farm was raided early in the war by the Hughes Regime. However, he has since played the game to keep his farm and provide for the local people as well as having the hidden agenda of resistance. His refusal to give us a turkey was an interesting twist.

"I'm fed up!" Mr. Smith told us. "I don't have to play this game anymore. I am ready to sacrifice all of this to get our freedom back."

Mr. Smith had a force of three hundred resistance fighters. Cowboy and I have hit a gold mine in the heart of this storm.

Mr. Smith and his wife Mabel offered us a warm bed for two nights while we discussed options. The Smith's had no idea that most of Florida and everything west of the Mississippi River was free and held governmental accountability. We explained that an operational government was being created and that once in place it would be ready to take over Washington, replace the regime and set the process in motion to establish a new congress and democratic nation.

Cliff Smith and his wife Mabel had tears in their eyes when they heard this news. With that news the Smith's began to tell us something we didn't know. Cliff Smith revealed a rumor that he heard that Paul and Janet Blair were hiding Hughes in their home. If this were true it would open the opportunity for Cowboy and me to assassinate Hughes.

On a clear but cool morning we thanked Mr. Smith and his wife for the warm beds and their hospitality. They told us they would be standing by. He then graciously gave us two fresh large turkeys and sent us back to D.C. It had been quite a productive journey.

By the time we arrived back at Ford's residence it was nearing nightfall. A few gun shots rang out in the distance causing onlookers to peak out from behind their window shades. Cowboy and I surprised Nicole with the turkeys as she granted us access to her large home and kitchen area.

"Good Lord! How did you come about getting those large turkeys?" Nicole asked. "Cowboy poured on his Texas charm and a pretty girl just handed them over." I said with a chuckle.

"I can believe that, but maybe I really don't want to know."

Nicole took the large turkeys and put them into her large freezer. "Won't the Blair's be surprised!" she said.

"Yes, they will." I said under my breath.

Cowboy and I made our way to our shelter behind the home with smiles on our faces. On the way we collected some firewood and brought it to our savior called a franklin stove and lit a warming fire. Cowboy pulled out his whiskey flask and took a swig.

"Where do you continue getting liquor Cowboy?" I asked.

"Janet" He replied with a grin.

"Are you? Never mind." I said.

I shook my head and smiled at Cowboy as we planned out our next move. Thanksgiving Day was six days away. We had been invited to the Blairs for Thanksgiving Day to help with chores and then they were gracious enough to have us eat with them. I think Janet convinced Paul that we were the Thanksgiving charity case, being Christian and all.

The fire was burning bright and warm that night. My head was spinning with thoughts of a renewed America. Cowboy lay snoring away with his ten-gallon hat perched on his faced. What finally put me to sleep was a relaxing thought of Emma. I wondered where she was and if she thought of me. I looked forward to the day of being in the Florida sunshine once again and sitting on the shore with her.

The following week flew by rather quickly. Cowboy and I committed to our chores for our keep and kept to ourselves. A lone young boy found us the day before Thanksgiving with word from Cliff Smith. He simply said, "Everything is a go." And walked away.

Thanksgiving Day was rather warm comparatively. Cloudy skies seem to forecast what was to come.

"Stay focused Bo." Cowboy said.

I was. It was time to play my part to change history.

Thanksgiving Day arrived. The Blair home was extravagant. Even in the worst of times the home had elegant furnishings, large rooms, chandeliers that hung high from the ceiling. Bodyguards and men surrounded the area. With electricity in Washington D.C. being a luxury, this home had it all.

As we approached the front doorway we were searched carefully by well-dressed large men. We were greeted by Janet at the door as she gave myself and Cowboy a quick hug and I could have sworn I saw her wink at Cowboy. On the left side of the hallway entrance was a large room with a very large formal dining table decorated in amazing fashion. She asked that we follow her to a separate room where two men stood at each side of the doorway.

"Gentlemen thank you for joining us. Paul and I really appreciate all that you have done for us, and we want to show our appreciation. Please take a seat. Paul will come say hi momentarily. Our other guests will arrive shortly."

Cowboy and I took a seat in the adjacent room next to the formal room.

"Focus Bo." Cowboy said.

"Not a problem Cowboy, this is perfect."

We anticipated every move and with heads up from Janet, we acted accordingly. Janet and Nicole knew nothing of our military background. They knew nothing of our plans. They simply were appreciative that we saved their lives one day and were looking for a better America. As we sat patiently waiting, we were served a glass of wine along with a small dish of hors D' oeuvres. Cowboy smiled and took a sip of wine as he offered me a toast.

"Focus Cowboy." I said.

We could hear as several people arrived and were escorted to the formal main dining room.

"I guess we get the kids table this year." Cowboy said with a grin. I smiled back.

"Well hello Bo and Tobey." Nicole said as she stuck her head in to make her presence known.

"Nicole, good to see you and look amazing." I said. "Thank you, Bo and happy Thanksgiving, to both of you." "Yes! Happy Thanksgiving."

Several candles were lit around the room and the chandelier hanging above us over the table was dimmed to create an atmosphere.

"Gentlemen I just wanted to come in and say hello! Tobey, please remove your hat."

It was Paul Blair. He made short, small talk and quickly retreated and then came into the room with a surprise guest. As he entered the men standing inside the doorway ordered us to "Please stand!" We followed their instructions as Cowboy quickly removed his Cowboy hat. As we stood a man walked into the room standing tall at the doorway.

"Gentlemen may I introduce the President of this great country, Mr. Gerald Hughes." Paul Blair said.

The rumors were true, and Cliff Smith was right. He's been under our nose the whole time. We greeted our nemesis with smiles and gratitude so as not give away our disdain.

It's very nice to meet you sir." I said as I reached to shake his hand. He refused my handshake and only said a brief "Happy Thanksgiving" as he turned away and left the room.

Cowboy and I sat back down and looked at each other. Cowboy couldn't help but grin. I took a sip of wine.

I have to say that my life has often been blessed with opportunities, but this is amazing. I found myself thinking of Sarge and what he would say to me right now. What would he do?

"Stay focused Bo." Cowboy said.

I lifted my wine glass to toast. "Should be anytime." I said.

A young lady entered our room and asked us to join her in the Lord's prayer. She was no more than sixteen, beautiful and well dressed.

We acknowledged her and complied by folding our hands and bowing our heads.

"Our Father, who art in Heaven, Hollowed be thy name, Thy Kingdom come, thy will be done, On earth as it is in Heaven…"

That was as far as she got before the first explosion went off. It rocked the large home and blew in the glass in the main dining room. The young girl fell to her knees. Cowboy grabbed his table knife as planned and cut the throat of one of the guards at the doorway as he fell down on his knees. I did the same to other guard. Warm blood covered my hands. We quickly made our way to the main dining area where the guests were beginning to stand up stunned. The second explosion went off in the rear of the house and sent debris flying down the long hallway. Cowboy and I quickly executed Paul Blair and Gerald Hughes before people knew what was happening. I grabbed a small handgun from Paul Blairs jacket and began firing at the approaching guards trying to enter the home. Simultaneous gunfire erupted outside by Cliff Smith's resistance fighters giving us cover to escape. I looked back to find Cowboy.

"I had to go back in for my hat!" he stated with a grin as he ran from the residence. Two resistance fighters on motorcycles pulled up and asked us to hop on. We complied and they sped away with us leaving the battle to ensue.

A small farmhouse was to the south of Capitol Poultry. It was the home of Mabel and Clifford Smith. All was quiet and Mrs. Smith had a dinner prepared in our honor.

"You had to go back in for your hat!?" I asked. Cowboy just grinned has he tilted up his flask to take a swallow.

"Cowboy that damn hat of yours causes more trouble than its worth!" I said, putting my hand on his shoulder.

"If only you'd seen what that hat has seen."

Chapter Twelve

Hero's

We hid out on the property of Capitol Poultry for two days. Cliff Smith and his wife were extremely hospitable. Mr. Smith briefed us on the fighting that ensued with his men. He lost three good men in the fighting, but the head of the snake has been cut off. The Hughes Regime was now without its leader and second in command. Cowboy and I were now well rested and had a meet up with a boat at Potomac Park that will take us out to meet up with our ride home.

There is something I'll miss about this mission. The weather was cold, we had sleepless nights, times when we thought our cover was blown, fights, and the feeling of being an indentured servant, but we also met some nice people in an unfortunate situation. We never saw Janet or Nicole again. Mr. Smith said he last saw them crying over the bodies of their dead husbands. Sometimes the cost of war comes home to those that carry the sword.

We jumped on some horses and made our way unobstructed to the Potomac Park and met a young boy about twenty years old eager to take us down the Potomac to Chesapeake Bay where we will transfer to a larger vessel to take us back to Key West.

"You know you're hero's, right?" The young man asked.

I smiled at the boy and asked him his name.

"My name is Brian, sir."

"Brian, we appreciate your sentiment, but we are just men that happen to be in the right place at the right time to serve our country." I told him.

"Speak for yourself Bo! I'm a hero son, don't ever forget that!" Cowboy said with a laugh as he patted the young man's shoulders.

"Let's get out of here shall we!" Cowboy said.

The boat was an older model version of a former water taxi that was used currently to take people to and from different places for markets and bartering. We seem to blend into the scenery so as not to cause any undue attention. It was hard to gauge the sentiment of the local people, but most seemed unaware of the assassination of Hughes and Blair. The confusion of Hughes militia was apparent. We saw areas that were once heavily fortified that were now left unprotected. If there was to be another uprising, we didn't see any signs of it.

By late afternoon we were in the wide-open bay area. As the boat made its way through the choppy dark water the wind whipped around us, and the cold sea spray hit our faces. Brian kept his focus on his task and looked the part of a brave sea captain. I had a stick of beef jerky that Mabel had given me before we left her home. I took it out of my pocket and handed it to Brian.

"It's not much my friend but please take it."

Brian was very appreciative and smiled. Small things were often luxuries in these times. As I looked out to watch the sun setting, I thought of better days to come. I asked myself what could possibly be next. I was looking forward to a warm day at the beach.

"Well, I'll be damned!" Cowboy said. "Look at that!"

I looked toward the horizon and made out a ship we were heading directly toward.

"Holy shit! Is that the Dreadnaught?"

I shifted in my seat and stood up to get a better look.

"Cowboy, I do believe that is the Dreadnaught!"

"She looks like the old rust bucket I remember!" Cowboy said.

We were excited to see that lovely lady again no matter how rusty she looked. As we got closer no less than forty men and women were on deck cheering us as we approached.

"I told you we're heroes!" Brain yelled with a smile.

Cowboy lifted his hat high above his head and began waving it. The crew cheered us on as we came close and boarded. I gave Brian a hug and thanked him for his passage. Cowboy gave him his flask of whiskey with a strong handshake. I watched as Brian maneuvered his boat away and gave a wave and a thumbs up to us. We were greeted warmly by Captain Surles, Quin, and Irish.

"You remember your comrades?" Captain asked with a big grin.

"Irish you sloppy old dog! How are you doing buddy?" Cowboy asked.

"We were picked up two weeks ago waiting on you slackers! I heard you two had a nice Thanksgiving!" Quin said with a laugh as he gave me a hug.

"You two are the heroes! We were bored, caught in the middle of a family cattle drive, and were attacked by bandits! What a shit show!" Irish said.

"We will have to catch up! It's so good to see you guys." I said.

Cowboy and I were walked through the ship to the mess hall when I asked Quin the obvious question.

"Is Emma here?"

"I don't think so Bo, I haven't seen her."

Irish overheard me ask. "She's not here lover boy. I've been all over this ship looking for a pretty face and I haven't seen her."

I relaxed with the boys in the mess hall having yet another fine meal. I was so happy to be aboard the Dreadnaught, but disappointed Emma was not here. It's been close to a year since I've seen her and have had minimal correspondence. I suppose I should put the thought of her in my past. I hoped she was doing ok.

Cowboy and I found our old bunks and slept well that night. The old ship swayed from side to side with the motion of the ocean rocking me to an easy and soundful sleep I haven't had in a while. We've been told that shortly after we left, armies surrounded Washington and took back many of the governmental offices. I look forward to hearing the complete report once back in Key West.

It was a quick two- and half-day cruise back to Key West. Once again, our mission was greeted by cheering onlookers and welcomers hearing of our daring mission and success in bringing an end to the

Hughes Regime. It hasn't quite hit me yet that I am now a part of history. Being a hero doesn't settle well with me. The mission was a success, but it didn't come without sacrifice. The men we killed were tyrants yet the time we spent getting to know their wives, their friends, their homes, their lives is personal. I have very bitter feelings about this war. The lives it took, the sacrifices that were made on both sides. My sacrifices, my Olivia, my father, my mother, my friends. It is sometimes easy to find myself believing that it is all for nothing. When I looked into the eyes of the young man that risked his life to take Cowboy and I from Washington D.C. out to the Dreadnaught I know that there is hope. It is not for nothing. It is for something, something very special. Our democracy is very fragile. Like a delicate flower that can be crushed without care. It takes strong people, men, and women of all kinds to make a democracy work. I am finding that I am so proud to be a part of something that is so much bigger than myself.

Captain Surles led Cowboy, Quin, Irish, and me off the ship as we were greeted first by Lt. Beck and the now Lieutenant Harrison. It was great to see the men that took me in and made me a soldier. Harrison looked great and was hugged by all of us standing strong and returning a strong hug. I looked into his eyes. This was the man that I looked up to like no other. It was so good to see him. Next to him was Commander Bell and then General Bishop. Each man shook our hands with strength and greeted us with "Congratulations".

"Please follow me Gentlemen." General Bishop said. We followed the General to the Monkey House, each of us smiling from ear to ear. Cowboy with his ten-gallon hat blocking the bright south Florida sun, Irish and Quin looking as if they had just won the lottery and myself wondering how I got here.

I awoke to a beam of sunshine peering through the old jalousie windows in my room. My sleepy eyes focused upon the ceiling fan slowly turning above me. "Nice to have electricity." I thought to myself. I turned my head to the side and saw the Distinguished Service Cross on my night table beside me. An honor bestowed upon Cowboy and I the evening before. "The tide is turning in this war." I thought to myself. What an incredible honor it was to be a part of such an event in such an incredulous time. I sat up in my bed feeling rested from a good night's sleep. I dressed and walked out to see Cowboy, Quin and Irish sitting around a small table talking incessantly to catch up. Our brotherly bond made us inseparable. Cowboy wearing his medal upon is bare chest like the war hero he is. They were all smiles.

"Good morning, gentlemen!" I said. "I know you're not talking to Cowboy!" Irish said, always the joker. I smiled along with men and poured myself of glass of fresh orange juice from the oranges that were picked from the backyard tree.

"What's on the agenda men?" I asked.

"We're headed over to the Monkey House to say our goodbyes to the Sarge. You coming?" Cowboy asked. "Of Course." I said.

The day was beautiful, almost reminiscent of better times. Hope had meaning on this day. A short briefing by Colonel Hatcher to the Key West Army contingent was followed by our goodbyes to our fearless leader Lieutenant Harrison.

"Captain Tony's?" Cowboy asked. "Captain Tony's it is!!" Irish replied.

Chapter Thirteen

<u>Spring</u>

To say that Spring renews hope is an understatement after war. The war had been declared over by May following our mission. The General offered Cowboy, Quin, and me another mission that involved going to the west coast. Cowboy and I declined but Quin took him up on the offer and headed west. We felt we had a better opportunity of being part of the cleanup action on the east coast. Danny and Brenda moved back to Connecticut hoping to find and reconnect with other family members. The Dreadnaught remained in Key West, but Captain Surles did not. He retired and left the service to join rebuilding efforts in his hometown of Jacksonville Florida.

Although the war had been declared over after six long years of fighting the rebuilding of infrastructure and government institutions became the new challenge. Fringe groups of the Hughes Administration's freedom fighters were scattered across the country and declared terrorists by the interim government. An election was planned for November, and many found solace in the fact that America, as it once was, was on a comeback.

The Army became solidified once again and a Joint Chiefs of Staff was created to form a national defense force that represented the unionized United States. Not unlike our forefathers that created a country out of colony's, it is an amazing process to watch as local communities came together to build the country into a Union once again. Delegates and leaders came together in Washington D.C. to form new legislation and help fund infrastructure projects throughout the newly governed States. The politics of the past that became so divisive and broken were resigned to be redeveloped into new political parties that held closer to our founding fathers' beliefs of freedom and strength through unity rather than division. Communication was found to be at the forefront of having a strong Union.

I was approached by my new commanding officer Lieutenant Colonel Jacob Allen to join a division that would be creating a National Communications Team to observe and suppress misinformation that could be coming from existing rebel groups, foreign countries, and other adverse groups that could influence rebuilding efforts. Although my time with the Army was wearing on me, I enjoyed being at the forefront of a nation rebuilding. I jumped at the chance. The brotherhood of Cowboy, Quin, Irish and me would always be on my mind and the men remained dear to my heart. Cowboy decided to leave the Army and go into business for himself and was joined by Irish. How these two men ended up working together is beyond me. Cowboy was reunited with his horse Tabasco, and they happily live on a farm outside of Austin Texas where he fits right in running a stable. Irish lived not far from Cowboy and began dating a lovely Mexican girl named Maria. I never saw those two men again although I will never forget the sacrifices we made together.

I had to leave the paradise of the Florida Key's behind and move to the Washington D.C. area specifically Alexandria Virginia. I reported to the Pentagon to officially receive my assignment. The war had taken its toll on the Capital area, but I was familiar with the landscape since the last time I was here, although it was for very different reasons.

I found it comforting that Alexandria managed to have power back although blackouts were still common. I managed to secure living quarters in a rather modest apartment just on the outskirts of Alexandria. A regular paycheck now made life much easier to predict. The two-bedroom apartment was on the second floor of a two-story complex built just before the war. It had some war damage but overall, it was in good condition. A few days of settling in slipped by and I found myself eager to get to work on my new duties and become a team leader.

My first day to report to work had finally arrived. I opened a large door to a rather luxurious brick building in downtown Alexandria that somehow appeared to escape the ravages of war. As I walked in the large room, the air felt moist, and the scent of mold was in the air as if I entered an ancient space. The ceilings were high and the sounds of my boots on the hard floor seemed to echo through the large lobby. A beautiful young lady standing behind a large reception desk greeted me with a smile.

"May I help you?"

"Hi yes, my name is Bo Brown and I have an appointment with Russell Taylor."

The young lady quickly picked up the phone and called Mr. Taylor. Service with a smile.

"Lieutenant Brown?" I heard my name and quickly turned.

I saw a young man walking from the elevator dressed smartly and reaching out to shake my hand.

"Lieutenant Brown, I've heard great things about you. Welcome! I am Russell Taylor, and I am so happy to meet you."

"Thank you, you aren't Army?" I asked as he walked me to the elevator.

"No Sir, I'm a civilian contractor working on behalf of the Army to assist with the communication project you will be leading. We are excited to have you and getting started."

"Ok, please call me Bo." I said.

Although I was still technically in the Army, I suppose my new role would be mainly civilian in function. I was a supervisor over a selected group of civilians each contracted to work for the Army. The Army just wanted their fingers involved with the oversite of national communications, the upstart of social media and I suppose what is deemed misinformation. I'm already finding this job fascinating.

I found myself in a room of sixteen eager staff members gazing at me as if I was their savior. Most were young but a few of the individuals had a look about them that I could recognize as battle hardened. All were weary of war, and a few were so young when the war began, they barely knew anything of life as it was before the war.

I gathered the group and began telling them a little about myself.

"Good morning. My name is Bo Brown. I'm originally from West Virginia, worked in New York City, but like many of you I was displaced by the war and found myself in some interesting places. I am glad to be here, and I am glad you all are here. We have an important task to perform. We will perform that task as a team. As you all know broadband services are beginning to come back online and with that there will be a lot of social media activity and some of that social media activity will be nefarious. Our job is to seek out that nefarious activity and suppress it. There is a new organization that has been created out of the Freedom Party Regime and they call themselves the Black Angels. We will be monitoring this group as well as a few others to undermine their nefarious activity that includes none other than misinformation aimed at the upcoming election as well as misinformation regarding policy, appointments, health care and education. Ladies and gentlemen, we are the point of the spear in assuring that the rebuilding of this country's foundations goes as smoothly as possible. I don't have to tell you that it was a campaign of misinformation and lies that got Gerald Hughes into power. With that said, I have been asked to protect this country's liberties and freedom of speech. So how do we do that while trying to suppress nefarious organizations' speech? That, my good team, is our challenge."

Such an interesting place I find myself in now. I'm leading a team of dedicated professionals committed to overseeing the rebuilding of communication services and activities in a newly forming United States of America. Only eight years ago I was working at a prestigious accounting firm as a Financial Analyst in New York City. I was happily married to a beautiful lady with a supportive family that lived on a beautiful farm in West Virginia and surrounded by fun lively friends. In hindsight, I was living the dream. War brings loss, heartache, pain, and broken dreams. Today, I find myself at a new beginning, but it's not just me. There is an entire country of people that are just like me. People searching for lives again, searching for hope and searching for loved ones that may not exist any longer. You may think this is the end of my story, but no, this is just the beginning.

Chapter Fourteen

<u>Fall</u>

It was exciting yet formidable to have full access to broadband again. The internet was up and running, people walked the streets again gazing at their cell phones and business and manufacturing activity was booming. I often spoke to Cowboy and Irish who were living the life in Texas and apparently running quite a large ranch down there. I lost touch with my old friend Quin but the last time I heard from him he informed me that our old buddy Austin, from Harcroft & Harrison was killed in the war. His widow Francesca escaped to California and that was the last he heard from her. Life at times is like a revolving door of friendships, loss, and pain. I have a new team now that gave me focus and new friends.

Charlie Adleman was one of those guys that was a little off, but everybody seemed to enjoy. Charlie took no shit from anyone, and I think people admired him for that. He was one of those guys that you always knew where you stood. He was a bit younger than me but saw a lot of fighting during the war. Looking at him, he didn't appear to have the strength of a soldier but from the stories I've heard he was quite the hero in his own right. He is slender, tall, with a mop of brown hair that never seemed to be combed and wore glasses that never seemed to fit him right. I've heard him described as a skinny Clark Kent that took no shit. That description seemed to fit.

With Fall brought the elections of new Congress and a new President. The interim government run by General Bishop and his staff was doing a good job. I thought that he was succeeding in the rebuilding of the infrastructure of our country as well as renewing allies with foreign governments. He was the leading candidate for President as a Democrat but there were several other contenders from the Republican Party as well as a few Independents. It was an interesting time in our country's history, and it kept my Team very busy with quelling the onslaught of a misinformation campaign by foreigners as well as domestic actors.

"Bo, you got a minute?" Charlie asked as he stuck his moppy head in my office. I always left my door open for staff.

"Of course, come on in Charlie."

"So, I guess I need to make sure this is ok with you, or I suppose I should say this organization we are working for."

"What is Charlie?" I asked.

"Well, I'm fucking Natasha."

"You mean Natasha, the receptionist downstairs?"

"Yes sir." He replied.

"Well, that's great Charlie, congratulations!" I said.

"Yes Sir it's kind of after the fact but since we are getting kind of serious, I thought I'd let you know." Charlie said with a grin.

"Well, she is a very attractive young lady and I'm happy for you Charlie."

"Can I ask you something else Bo?"

We seemed to be on a first name basis now.

"Of course!" I said.

"Would you join a few of us out for a beer sometime?"

Not only did I accept the offer from Charlie, but I told him I would pay.

"Let's go now! Gather the staff and let's get out of here!" I said.

Charlie looked at me like I had lost my mind. "I'm serious! Get Natasha and whomever else feels like doing some day drinking and let's go!" I said with an awkward smile.

There is something to be said about an offer from your team mates to socialize on a personal level, especially if they invite you. The offer made me reflect on how the war has affected me. I started questioning whether my personal relationships were not personal in nature at all but just professional. It seems in my dedication to making a better world, I had become consumed with nothing but working and letting my personal side slip away. It was time to change that.

"Hey everybody, as boss of this place I would like today to be a day of getting to know each other! We're getting out of this building and going bar hopping! To those that don't drink, you're welcome to come anyway!"

I've never seen my staff look so surprised. A few started to smile, a few just looked dumbfounded.

Charlie threw down a binder he was holding and said, "Fuck it! Let's go! We've been together eight months people let's get out and have a little fun!"

O'Shaughnessy's Pub was a long-time staple in Alexandria Virginia. It closed for several years during the war and served as an outpost for resistance fighters. I became familiar with the place during my time here with Cowboy. It was now back open and a proud member of the Alexandria bar scene although like many businesses it now has strict rules for entering.

Kaitlyn Summers was a very energetic forty-year-old that was selected to be on my team by the reunification committee. The reunification committee selects individuals from around the country for infrastructure and reunification projects in the rebuilding process. She is smart, witty, and focused and once served on the administration at Harvard in the School of Communications.

Russell Taylor, the man that introduced me to this Team was selected to be my right-hand man and used to work for Microsoft as a Communications Engineer before the war. Although Microsoft went silent during the war it has managed a comeback, but Russell has agreed to stay on with us. He is smart, loyal and loves being a part of this Team.

Bob Sanders is a war veteran as most of us are but before that he led a team of threat detection engineers for IBM. He is forty-three and lost his family to the Delta Gang. He had a wife and three daughters. He mostly keeps to himself but enjoys working with the team and being a part of rebuilding America.

Kyle Shepherd is the son of a war hero. As the youngest on the Team at twenty-seven, he was selected to be on my team as a favor to his father, but I find him very helpful, although not a real intellectual he still brings an advantage to the team. Kyle is from Kansas and was mostly distant from the fighting of the war.

Natasha Graham serves as the building receptionist. She is a beautiful young lady at twenty-six years old with ambitious goals. She is the apple of Charlies eye.

Of the sixteen staff members that I oversee these individuals along with Charlie accompanied me to O'Shaughnessy's. Discussions ranged from the weather during the battle of Charleston to the milk industry in West Virginia to how our communication efforts were impacting the country.

"Kyle, I never met your father, but I heard he was a very good soldier. I'm sorry for your loss." I said to Kyle.

"Thank you, Sir. He was a great man, and we miss him a lot. My Mother still struggles but she seems to do better each day."

I knew Kyle's father Ben Shepherd died in a fierce clash with the Freedom Party Regime just outside Washington D.C. in the early days of the war. He defended himself and several others against a raid of over one hundred men. Kyle and his mother waited out the war in Kansas with several other family members.

"I appreciate you Lieutenant Brown and I think you and the team are doing a great job here." Kyle said.

"Kyle you're part of this team and I appreciate you! Now, go grab another beer!" I replied to him with a smile.

The bar and the company were very reminiscent of times past. Looking around at the custom wood bar, the lighting, the smiles, and laughter made me smile. I haven't felt this way in a long time, and it wasn't all the alcohol.

As the team chatted with each other I became comfortable on an old wooden stool that I surmised had survived the war. I watched a man at the bar staring into space with a glass of whiskey on ice. He was elderly and he had the look of pain on his face. He was obviously trying to drink his dark memories away. Sad, I thought. It took me back several years to a man named Thomas that I met walking in the road during the war. A man I never got to know, and I couldn't save from blood thirsty gangs but how I wish he were here with me now to finish our long-ago conversation.

What happened next can't be made up. Although the bar was dark, the figures I saw walking toward me were very familiar. One was the beautiful Natasha and the other I thought was a figment of my imagination.

"Lieutenant I'd like to introduce you to someone." Natasha said, however, the person needed no introduction. She had the most beautiful red hair I had ever seen, and I would recognize those eyes anywhere.

"This is..."

"Emma!" I interrupted, hardly believing my eyes. I took a hard swallow.

By the look on her face, she couldn't believe her eyes either.

"Oh my God! Bo!?" She said. Her smile lit up the room.

If my feet were touching the ground, I couldn't tell. I looked upon her beautiful face in wonderment.

"Where the hell have you been?" I asked practically breaking out in a sweat.

We hugged with a tight embrace that I had been waiting for, for a long time. My arms wrapped around her with a sweet embrace that I never thought I'd feel again. I enjoyed the feel of her arms around me.

"Oh my God, Emma the nurse!"

"Bo, I can't believe this! I was a good friend to Natasha's mother Alice. When Alice was killed, I was there for Natasha. I had no idea."

"My mother was a nurse as well." Said Natasha, "But I no idea you two knew each other. Emma is like a second Mom to me."

I felt like a sixteen-years-old again, smiling nervously.

"How long has it been Bo?" Emma asked.

"Um, I don't know. The last time I saw you, you left on the Dreadnaught. I was in Key West. I served and completed several missions. The Dreadnaught sailed me back to Key West after a mission, but you were not on her. This is crazy Emma. It's so good to see you."

"Hey asshole want another beer?" an interruption from Charlie.

"HEY! LUETINANT BO!" Charlie yelled as I was obviously entranced.

I couldn't take my eyes off her.

"No more beer for me Charlie, but thanks for the offer." I said while still staring at Emma. Emma gave a sheepish smile.

"What do you mean offer? You said you were paying!" Charlie barked back.

"Yea, yea, Charlie no problem, help yourself." I said.

I must get my wits about me and get myself together.

"Hey, everyone, I want to introduce you to someone." I said to the group as I put my arm around Emma.

"This is Emma Ford. She is a dear friend of mine, and she is the best nurse in the world!" I said with a smile.

Emma smiled from ear to ear as I took her by the arm to lead her to a small private area to catch up. This day suddenly became a wonderous occasion.

The small table was candlelit, which only accentuated Emma's fair complexion and green eyes. She possesses a captivating and unique charm, and her confidence radiates through her striking appearance.

"It's so good to see you, Emma." I said.

"I must say, I thought about you a lot when I left Key West." She said.

"Emma, I wrote you."

"I must tell you something Bo. First, I knew you were here, in Alexandria, and I debated coming to see you."

I listened intently.

"Not long after I left, I met a man. A soldier, much like you Bo, and I wasn't ready for a relationship when I met you. But I must say that you gave me the courage and the confidence to perhaps attempt love. I saw things differently after you and I thought about you often."

I remained focused on her every word as I listened.

"I fell in love. His name was Norman. He was a kind man, a good man. We met on the dreadnaught as he was preparing for a mission."

"Was?" I asked.

"He completed several successful missions with only a few scratches, and I decided to leave with him. I left the Dreadnaught to live with him and his son Jordan in Savannah Georgia. There was a safe area near Savannah as the war began to wind down and we were living contently. We assumed there were plenty of defense forces surrounding the area. Like you he volunteered with the Army but because of Jordan he wanted a homelife, or the best life he could provide due to the circumstances. Jordan was only six at the time. Norman was gunned down while he was splitting wood outside our apartment just before Christmas two years ago. Jordan and I hid in a safe room. I guess it wasn't a clear and safe area after all. It was hard on me Bo. I'm so tired of losing people and seeing people hurt."

"I'm so sorry Emma. You can't blame yourself."

"I don't blame myself. I blame this fucking war." She said.

"And Jordan?" I ask.

"Jordan is now with his grandmother. His mother was killed in the war early on. He's a good boy Bo."

"I'm very sorry Emma. This war has taken a lot of good people from us. You said you weren't sure you wanted to see me?"

"Yea, I don't know. I do, I do want to see you and I am so happy you are ok and I'm here with you now."

I reached across the table and took Emma's hands. "I'm so sorry, God, I missed you, Emma."

My mother called me a dreamer. I appreciated the sentiment from her but to continuously dream of something may mean you never achieve the dreamy goal. Maybe she meant I was imaginative or optimistic and had ambitious ideas. Or perhaps she thought I let my mind wander into fantasies. Whatever she meant I suppose in some respects she was right. My life up to this point has been a series of fortunes and misfortunes. I've been fortunate to have a wonderful family and fine experiences but unfortunate to have lost them. Whatever dreams that I may have had prior to the war were stripped of me and I was forced into slavery of the time. I was fortunate to survive. My life has now been recreated into the form of a leader. I enjoy it. The fact that Emma has entered back into my life suggests that life is not always free will. Perhaps there is an undertone of predetermined events. Perhaps Quin was right. Perhaps there were conspiracies that led to the overtaking of the government. Perhaps Thomas was meant to die in my house. Perhaps I was meant to meet Emma on the Dreadnaught. Perhaps the bullets that nearly missed me had a predetermined path. I suppose one would never know.

Chapter Fifteen

<u>Resumption</u>

Cynthia Pichette left a small apartment in the southwest part of Boston, climbed in her car, and drove approximately seventeen hours to a Federal Office Building in Atlanta Georgia. The new Federal Building was a gleaming example of the regrowth and reconstruction of the after-war period. Housed in this building, named after famed civil rights leader Martin Luther King were numerous government offices including Housing and Urban Development, Federal Highway Reconstruction, and Education. Cynthia parked several blocks away among the large new buildings and strolled slowly toward the Martin Luther King Federal Building. As she walked, she gazed around her and waved to several children that were playing in a nearby church school yard. The heat of the day kept Cynthia's pace slow as she made her way to the front entrance of the building. She made her way in through the large revolving doors and began to step quickly. Security guards quickly took notice of Cynthia as she was wearing a very large coat on a hot summer day. Cynthia walked to the center of the lobby as she smiled at the people around her. Her hand withdrew her cell phone which appeared to be attached to another small mechanism. She pushed the button, and the lobby of the Martin Luther King Federal Building was consumed by an explosive force destroying most of the first floor of the building instantly causing the rest of the five-story building to collapse. This terrorist act cost two hundred and eighty-nine lives.

Cynthia Pichette was a thirty-five-year-old mother of four who identified herself as a true Christian. She had originally become intrigued by the postings in social media regarding the overtaking and demise of the Freedom Party of America. She became radicalized by joining a small group of sympathizers in her hometown in Massachusetts and felt the need to act upon those that were once again destroying America. It was never clear why she chose the Martin Luther King Building in Atlanta Georgia.

I often asked myself what sacrifices must be made by living in a free society with differing opinions and a diverse makeup of people and beliefs. It is these values that our country was built upon.

Ten years after the end of the war that has now become known as the Great Civil War, small factions of dissidents still exist. The United States has always had and will continue to have domestic terrorism. Fighting the root cause of these terrorists is the challenge. President Bishop turned out to be a great President and turned the nation around with his communication style, bipartisan wins, and an economic boom in rebuilding the Nation. The Great Civil War was in the history books and the United Stated of America has persevered.

I retired two years ago from the Army for which I will be forever grateful. I keep my Medal of Commendation and Distinguished Service Cross in shadow boxes upon my wall. I gaze at them every morning when I wake up. I consider myself a very lucky man that happened to be at the right place at the right time, whether it was predetermined or not. It didn't matter anymore. It was history in the making.

"Ready for a hike Bo?" Emma asked.

Autumn in the mountains of northern New Mexico is beautiful. The air was crisp, and leaves were falling foretelling the coming winter.

"I am ready my Darling." I had pet names for Emma, honey and darling were my favorites.

Emma and I married on a day similar to this in New England only a year after we reconnected. She continued to nurse in Alexandria for five more years before retiring. I was lucky to have her in my life. She guided me through a stressful time that took its toll on me. The team I had developed was great, but I was later accused of censorship and violating the First Amendment. Despite the times and influence social media had on society, overseeing a communications office was a tightrope walk. Society expects free speech through social media. However, where do you draw the line between free speech, protected speech, and pure hate to recruit and admonish our way of life. I was enjoying retirement after seven long years in that appointment.

I took Emma by the hand and led her down a small trail beside our cabin that leads to the valley below. The cool breeze was refreshing.

"Did you hear about the bombing in Atlanta Bo?" "I did" I replied.

"Are we going to be ok Bo?" "Of course, we are Emma."

"The only thing I want to concern myself right now is how much food we need to have when Irish and Cowboy come to visit for Thanksgiving."

"It's our turn this year?" Emma asked, knowing the answer.

I turned and smiled at her.

"You know how I feel about Cowboy." She said.

I laughed.

"You drink too much when you get around him." She said.

"Yea, well, I guess I do." I said, tempering myself.

"Let's make a deal, if I drink too much, Cowboy and I will do the dishes." I said.

Emma took my hand. "My back is killing me, Bo; I think we may have to make this a shorter hike."

"That's fine."

We stopped and took a rest on a bench I made that overlooked the distant hills.

"It looks as though rain may be coming." I said. Emma just nodded her head and we both looked upon the view.

"The energy is strong today, Bo."

One of the things I loved about Emma was her spiritual belief in a worldly energy. Not a God, not a religion but what I like to think of as a presence of love, space, time, and nature combined into a wholistic energy that feeds the soul. My understanding and study of many Native

Americans is their spiritual awareness was very similar. Using the earth and energy of the land to support and guide them.

"I think it's the time of year." I said.

She laid her head on my shoulder. I loved times like this. We have made a good life for ourselves.

"Do you ever wish we could have had kids of our own Bo?" Emma asked.

"Not necessarily Honey. I think we were lucky to get through this life on our own. Let alone having children." I said with a chuckle. "In a different world perhaps. But in a different world we may never have met. You fulfill me Emma and that's enough for me."

"We better get in, rain is coming." She said.

Cowboy and I Irish arrived for Thanksgiving on a cold afternoon.

"Do you know that man brought his horse Bo?"

I looked out the window and saw my old friend leading a horse from the back of a trailer that was hitch to his truck. Irish was gathering a few bags from the backseat.

"Welcome Gentlemen!" I said as I walked outside to greet them. I noticed Irish walking with a limp and Cowboy with his forever ten-gallon hat on his head, held tight to his horse.

"Gentlemen? Where the hell do you see gentlemen?" Irish said with his Irish accent I had missed.

"We are just a couple of old horse soldiers!" Irish said.

"Speaking of horse soldiers" Cowboy said. "This is Thunder. Tabasco had to put down a while back, so this beautiful beast is my new buddy."

"I'm sorry about Tabasco Cowboy, but Thunder is more than welcome and it's nice to meet your new beautiful horse."

After our greeting the men came in and gave Emma a hug. We then settled on the porch with a hot cup of coffee and a glass of Texas whiskey.

"Did you hear about Quin Bo?" Cowboy asked.

"No. What about Quin?"

"The poor bastard died." He said.

I wasn't quite sure how to take that news. It was sudden and heartbreaking. "What?" I asked. I've known Quintero Rodriquez aka Quin since I worked in New York with him at Harcroft & Harrison.

"I've been trying to reach him about visiting me. Oh damn, I didn't know." I said.

"He was pretty messed up from his war injuries Bo. He was never the same. There was no funeral, just a cremation. That's the way he wanted it."

I took a sip of whiskey and had nothing else to say. Another loss.

With that news we made the best of the rest of the weekend. Cowboy had a good time but over drank as Emma had predicted. I suppose we all did. Cowboy enjoyed riding his horse Thunder down the trail to the valley below while Irish sat and watch a few games of football. Emma and I shared the responsibilities of hosting; cooking, cleaning, picking up after the men. It was good to have American traditions back.

The weekend passed quickly and we once again said our goodbyes. Heartbroken to say goodbye and heartbroken about another loss.

I saw Tobey Longstreet aka Cowboy only one more time in my life as Emma and I once again hosted Thanksgiving. After that the drinking got the best of him and I was told he fell from Thunder and died on a trail. I suppose that's the way Cowboys like to die. The last time I saw Stan McKinley aka Irish was at Tobey's funeral. I never saw him again. Unfortunately, time has a way of erasing some of the friends we knew.

Emma and I had few friends. The team I worked with was just that, a work team. Most of the team distanced themselves from me once I was accused of violating the First Amendment. I answered to the new Congress for my violations and felt mostly vindicated afterwards although it meant retirement for me. Emma keeps to herself other than being by my side and that is the way she likes it.

So that's about it. That's my story. Emma and I are in our sunset years and more in love than ever before. We've had some regrets but overall, we feel we've lived a good life despite the circumstances. I'm just a man that by happen chance became a soldier. I never thought of myself as a hero; just someone who survived.

I was lucky to have met the love of my life three times. Once with my beautiful wife Olivia and twice with Emma. They were both perfect unions in very different ways under very different circumstances. My life seems to have been full of resumption and reinvention. The ending of one story and the beginning of another. After all, isn't that what life is all about?